HOW SHE FELL

MARTINA MONROE BOOK 7

H.K. CHRISTIE

KEEKSTAR
MEDIA

Copyright © 2022 by H.K. Christie

Cover design by Odile Stamanne

If you would like to use material from this book, prior written permission must be obtained by contacting the publisher at:

www.authorhkchristie.com

First edition: December 2022

ISBN: 978-1-953268-13-6

Dedicated to Ms. Taylor Swift

1

LORI

If someone had told me that, at eighteen, I would be engaged and a mother-to-be, I would have told them they were bonkers. Like lock 'em up nuts. But the universe had special plans for me. It had been scary when I learned I was pregnant, but knowing I would have him by my side eased the worry away.

Rummaging through Este and my closet, I searched for the right dress to wear for the proposal. The crimson fit and flare would be perfect. Plus, it would disguise my growing baby bump. I pulled it out, stepped in front of the mirror, and held the dress up to my body. The deep red against my tan skin would drive him wild. Pair the look with a dark lipstick, and it would be perfect for the most important night of my life.

A twinge in my belly made me grimace.

"Are you okay?"

"Must have been something I ate. I'm fine." Or the baby was unhappy about something. Baby needed to calm down. Its daddy was about to propose, and our life together would be wonderful.

Another cramp.

Este scrunched up her face. "Are you sure? Maybe you should cancel."

She worried too much and had for as long as I could remember. I often teased her that she'd been stressed out when we shared our mother's womb and that's why she'd entered the world two minutes before I had.

Este never trusted Freddie and wasn't as sure as I was that he wanted to meet tonight in order to propose. It was because she didn't know him like I did. "Nothing is stopping me tonight," I declared.

Este raised her brow at that, but I ignored her and dressed for the big night. With my look complete, I said, "What do you think?"

"Beautiful. But won't you get cold?"

She had a point. It was a warm summer day, but it was colder in Alameda, a quaint city along the San Francisco Bay, especially in the evening. I grabbed the red scarf Auntie Araceli had given me for Christmas. Wrapping it around my neck, I said, "How about now?"

"Great."

"Put yours on, so we can take a picture together!"

Este trudged over to the closet to grab her matching red scarf. Wrapped up, she took the camera from her backpack. "All right." She held out the camera, extended her arm, and snapped a few pictures of the two of us.

Giggling, I said, "Now it's perfect."

"Are you ready to go?"

"Almost. Take a picture of my naked left hand." I placed my hand on my chest and made a fake sad face.

She took the photo.

"Now, I'm ready."

Este had agreed to drive me to meet Freddie and to take pictures of the momentous occasion. I was too nervous to drive, so Este did the honors.

Once parked, I gave her a big squeeze, before saying, "Okay, now, take my picture. The last moment before I'm an engaged woman."

Este leaned over and pulled up her purse. Peering inside, she frowned. "I forgot the camera."

Bummer. I wanted pictures of Freddie and me after the proposal. "No worries. I guess you can go. Freddie can drive me home. Wish me luck."

The frown remained. "Lori, I have a bad feeling about this."

And she gave me that disapproving look she always did when she didn't agree with my actions, which had been quite frequent lately. She didn't approve of Freddie and my relationship, but I think it was because she didn't understand. Neither one of us had a serious boyfriend before—Freddie was my first. But I knew in my heart it would all work out. Este was going to feel so silly when I returned home with a sparkly diamond on my finger. I waved her off and headed for the bridge.

The streetlights illuminated the dark path. There wasn't a single person around. My heartbeat pounded as I approached the bridge. The roar of the choppy water below stopped me. And a pang shot in my gut. I tried to ignore my brain, which was trying to tell me the sudden onset of stomach discomfort was a sign. I wasn't superstitious like that, was I? Maybe Este was right. Maybe all of this was a little strange. Studying the scene, I wondered if I should turn back but continued anyway. When I reached the middle of the bridge, I gripped the railing, looking from left to right, wondering if he would show. The bridge was frigid to the touch, and a chilly breeze swam through my hair.

As I waited, a thousand thoughts whirled around in my mind. What would he say? Was I all wrong or would he bend down on one knee and open a ring box, asking me to be his bride? Boots on concrete sounded, and my heart rate sped up. A deep, familiar voice said, "Hey."

Relieved at the sight of him, I said, "Hey," not believing I had, for a moment, thought this was a bad idea. He was the father of my child. I loved him. This was romantic. The scene of our first kiss nearly six months ago. Our relationship hadn't been great, but when he'd learned I was having his child, things changed. He was loving and attentive.

He put his arms around me and squeezed me tight. Freddie stepped back and said, "Thank you for meeting with me. You're all I can think about since we spoke the other day. I'm sorry it took me so long to come around, but I had to be sure."

I nodded, as if I absolutely understood what he was saying to me. His features were unusually dark, with the only light spilling from the lamps above. I wanted to see all of him in the daylight. His sparkling ocean blue eyes and paper-white smile. But as I had learned during our relationship, he had to do things his way and in his own time. "I missed you."

"I missed you too, and I've given us a lot of thought. I love you and want to be with you." He glanced down.

This was the moment I thought he was going to pull out a ring, but he said, "I think it's best if we don't have the baby so that we can move forward."

My chest constricted. "That's what you wanted to talk about?"

"I think it's what's best for both of us. We have our whole lives ahead of us. It's just not the right time for a baby, don't you think?"

Of course, it wasn't how I had planned, but everything until that point in our relationship seemed like fate. "No, I didn't plan on this happening right now, but I believe we can make it work. It might be rough the first couple of years, but eventually, we'll both have good jobs and a great life. It'll be wonderful. I promise."

"I don't think so. But I spoke with my parents, and they want to help. They'll take care of everything financially, plus give you a little extra to help out."

I could barely breathe and was trying my hardest to not cry. "Are you sure?" And what did he mean by a little extra? Were they trying to buy me off?

His eyes grew darker than before. "I'm absolutely sure. Please, just do this. For me. For us."

How could I respond to that? What did he mean? "I love you and our baby."

"This is how it has to be. I'm sorry."

He was sorry? Anger and hurt seared through my body. "How could you do this to me? I thought you said you were okay with the baby? You said it was my choice."

"I need you to promise you'll get rid of it and never discuss this with anyone. In exchange, I'll give you ten thousand dollars. That's a lot of money."

My world crashed down in the darkness, and I sobbed uncontrollably. He grabbed my shoulders. "Promise me."

Shaking my head, I said, "I can't believe you're doing this."

"Promise me. Please!"

"No!" I tried to break free of him, but he shoved me against the railing.

"You have to! Please! I'm begging you," he cried.

I screamed, "No!" As I clawed and punched at him, he picked me up, but I lost my balance and toppled over. A tug at my neck slowed me, but then it all happened so fast. With the wind whipping across my face, I heard a scream. Unsure if it was my own or someone else's, I flailed my arms and legs before crashing into the dark, murky water.

2

MARTINA

Staring at the stacks of banker's boxes filled with unsolved crimes reminded me of the very first case I worked with Hirsch and the Cold Case Squad. Three missing women spread across three different files. It was in that storage room I had connected them. When I had set out to pick a file, I had wanted to find and solve the most important case. Since then, I realized there wasn't a most important case because each person who went missing or died had a family and friends who thought they were the most important. So, how did we choose which case to take on next? Well, I knew one thing we had to do was to make sure we gave a voice to victims who were ignored or marginalized by society and determined not to be newsworthy. Stuffed in boxes, never to be thought of again by anyone other than the families and friends who missed them and would never know their fate. How to pick when there were too many? What I was looking for was the case that should've made headlines and would when we solved it. Glancing over at Vincent, I said, "You find anything?"

"There's an endless supply of missing persons and unsolved murders. How is it possible that so many cases remain unsolved?" Vincent sounded incredulous.

It was a common question people asked us. My mom's friends would visit the house and ask how there could be so many cold cases. They assumed, at some point, we would run out of work for the Cold Case Squad. But the devastating truth was that less than 60% of all murders in the United States were solved, along with thousands of missing persons cases that turned cold each year. Crimes weren't as easy to solve as many people liked to think. Missing persons were tricky, especially if the missing weren't reported right away or the original investigators had assumed because of their age, demographic, or lifestyle choices that they'd simply run away. Where did they run away to?

"That's why we're here."

Vincent smirked. "Yeah, and hopefully the next case will put us back in the sheriff's good graces."

Well, the sheriff couldn't like us any less. After Vincent's and my suspension, we both were on the sheriff's naughty list. Vincent was a full-time employee of the Sheriff's Department, whereas I was simply a contract investigator with an end date of December 31. It was May, which meant I had seven months to prove to the sheriff that he needed to keep me around. If not, there were worse things than returning to my firm and continuing to work private cases at Drakos Security & Investigations. During my suspension, I'd returned to the firm for a month. And I admit, it was easy to fall back into old routines working with my previous coworkers and a few fresh faces. But I missed working with Hirsch and Vincent and the rest of the squad. But this was one of those things in life that was out of my control, so I couldn't dwell on it, but I could try to do my best.

Although I agreed with Vincent that we needed to wow the sheriff and make him look good, to get him reelected, which was, from what I could tell, all he really cared about. Looking good. Staying in office. Power. Money. The usual roots of evil. There was no love lost between Sheriff Lafontaine and me, but he approved the funding for the Cold Case Squad, so I had to learn to smile, and nod, and do what I was told — most of the time.

With both hands, I grabbed a box from the stack and set it on the table. There was only one chair, and Vincent had occupied it as he studied a file. I lifted half the files from the box and set them on the table, then did the same with the second half.

So many files. It may not be a bad idea to assign someone to organize them.

I picked up the file on top, leaned against the wall, and read the few pieces of paper that concluded the missing teen was likely a runaway. Not even a photo of the missing girl was included. If I had a dollar for every cold case file that said it was a missing teen runaway that later turned out to be a kidnapping or murder, I'd have more than a few dollars. I set aside the file and picked up the next.

It wasn't much better. I was thinking there were some serious issues within the sheriff's departments. Half of the files had the most minimal of investigation and some not even the bare minimum. Between the light files and the fact Hirsch and I had found a few dirty cops during our investigations, I wondered if the issues remained or if new leadership had rid the department of the rotten apples.

Each time we picked out a new case, I wondered. Not that we always selected our cases, as we had learned the hard way. Sheriff Lafontaine had a lot of influence over what we investigated and what we didn't. I'd be lying if I said it didn't get on my nerves. A little time away had been a blessing.

With Hirsch on his honeymoon, I took some time off, too. Zoey had spring break, so we opted for a week in Southern California to play in the sand and visit Universal Studios and Disneyland. Zoey had a blast. Mom had a blast. I had a blast. The only one not pleased with the trip was Barney, our dog, who had to stay with Claire, Zoey's previous nanny. From what Claire reported, Barney had a great time at the dog park and running around her back yard, but it was clear he missed home, too. Upon our return, Barney greeted us with lots of slobbery kisses and a wagging tail.

The last few trips we had taken were to visit Disneyland, Zoey's choice, but I knew we should see more of our state, our country, and the rest of the world. My Zoey had never been out of the country or even out of the state. She was only ten years old, so I wouldn't expect her to be a world traveler yet, but I wanted to show her other cultures and places outside of California. It was a big world out there, and I wanted my girl to see it all. I had been lucky during my four years in the Army to see a good chunk of this Earth. Before we had Zoey, and when we were on leave, my husband Jared and I took weekend trips all around, up and down the west coast. We were young and a six-hour drive was no biggie. It was a different time.

Jared had been gone three years. In that time, my life had flipped upside down, then back up again. Our world looked different from before. I had a few more gray hairs and lines near my eyes, but we were okay. More than okay.

Mom moved in with us a few years back and helped take care of Zoey, which was a tremendous help when Zoey's nanny, Claire, left us to pursue a career in nursing. But things change. Zoey was getting older, and Mom was getting more serious with her boyfriend, Ted. The members of the Cold Case Squad called him Sarge. She and Sarge had certainly hit it off and had been going strong for quite a while now. Sometimes I wondered if they would move in together or get married. I didn't know what I would do without her help. But I supposed Mom didn't need to live with us to help with Zoey. Or I could hire a new nanny. Zoey had loved Claire but was understanding when

Claire graduated from college and became a nurse to help others.

We all have our gifts that God gave us. Mine was bringing closure to families and helping those who needed answers. Claire's was to help heal the sick. Mom acted as a sponsor to alcoholics new to their recovery. What would Zoey's be? Other than being the love of my life. I attempted to shake the thoughts away, needing to focus. I couldn't contemplate my girl growing up and heading to college and being on her own because it was bad enough she had started referring to me as 'Mom' instead of 'Mommy.' Time changes things, and, like it or not, we have to change with them.

Flipping through the next file, I did a double take. Literally. There were two missing persons who'd vanished twenty years before. I didn't remember hearing about the case twenty years ago. Although I would have been in my early teens, so not that surprising, I supposed. "Hey, Vincent."

Vincent put down the paper he was reading. He and I had become close over the last few months. He was a top-notch researcher and was becoming a keen investigator as well. Considering he and I conspired to break the rules together and therefore got punished together, we had a newfound under-standing of one another.

Our friendship wasn't something I would've predicted the first time we met. He was young and silly, but he'd proven to me and the rest of the squad that he was intelligent, hard-working, and always wanted to do what was right for the victims and their families. After the last few months, in my heart, I knew Vincent and Hirsch would always be my family. It was through hard times that your genuine friends were revealed. "Check this out." I handed him the report.

He looked over at me. "I don't get it. I mean, I'm too young to have seen any of this in the news, but..."

I pointed to the line on the intake form next to 'ethnicity.'

Vincent shook his head in disgust. "This is outrageous. How could this not have been splattered across the news? Don't answer that. I know the answer. They're not blonde, blue-eyed beauty queens."

"Exactly. Let's bring it to Hirsch."

3

HIRSCH

Vincent and Martina were chatting vigorously as they walked toward me with a file folder clutched in her hand. It had only been a week since I got back from my honeymoon — two weeks in Maui, and I barely remembered what the sea looked like or the beach or Kim in that little black bikini. No, I remembered Kim in that little bikini.

"What's that smile for?" Martina asked.

Martina and I were best friends, but I knew she didn't need to know all of my thoughts, especially about my beautiful wife. "What do you have there?"

"We found our next case."

"Okay." Although I was technically the Cold Case Squad leader, it was really Martina who ran the show. Nobody ever said anything. It was basically an understanding amongst all of us, including Martina. She usually got her way, one way or another. But to be fair, she was usually right, and even when she was wrong, she was a little right. It could be an asset, but it could also hurt us. I was still concerned the sheriff wouldn't renew her contract and wished we could turn things around. But I wasn't sure how. I was terrible at sucking up to the brass,

12

but I realized, for the good of the squad and my best friend, I would have to smooch Lafontaine's butt occasionally.

Martina and Vincent sat across from me.

I didn't know if it was a good thing that the two of them were conspiring on the next case, since they were already walking a pretty thin line with the sheriff. I was less concerned about Vincent than Martina. Not only was he young and could get a job pretty much anywhere, but I also doubted the sheriff would fire him. It's pretty difficult to fire an employee unless he broke the law, which some could argue he had. But it wouldn't make the sheriff look very good if he ousted one of our own.

Martina, on the other hand, was a contractor and nobody would know of her departure except for the squad. And I couldn't imagine doing this job without her. Not that I didn't have skilled investigators who worked tirelessly to bring closure to the families of victims and to find the missing. I did. But we started the squad together and it would be weird not to have her a part of it. Not only did I have to worry about Vincent and Martina, but the entire squad, a new wife, and hopefully a little one in the near future. "Let's have it."

Martina smiled. Time off had been good for her. "A missing persons case. Two, to be exact. Twin eighteen-year-old girls from San Ramon. They disappeared twenty years ago."

"Missing twins?"

"You don't remember hearing about them on the news?" Vincent asked.

"No." But I would think I would have. Missing twins would be a pretty big deal. They both looked at me like the punchline was coming. "They were born and raised in Louisiana but lived in California for a year before they went missing. Both college students. The family is originally from Honduras. They were reported missing by their aunt twenty years ago."

"Any suspects?"

Martina shook her head and pursed her lips. "Nope. The original investigator assigned to the case declared them... you want to guess?"

"Runaways?"

"Yep."

Vincent chortled. "We should start a jar. For every missing person labeled a runaway, we put in five bucks. At the end of the year, we have a pizza party."

"Not a bad idea." It was good to see Vincent in good spirits. "Is that the entire file?"

Martina said, "It is. No suspects. But no proper investigation either."

"When did the aunt report them missing?"

"She didn't report them for two days. She said she wasn't worried at first, but then when one of the sisters' employers called and said she hadn't shown up, the aunt realized it was time to be worried."

"And I'm guessing it was unusual for her to not show up for work?"

"Yes. Both girls, Esther and Loretta, were straight-A students enrolled in college, and Loretta worked part time. They shared one car and did almost everything together. They had moved to San Ramon the year before they started college."

"Where were they from originally?"

"New Orleans."

"What about the mom and dad?"

"Their mother had passed away the year before. It was why they moved to California. Father wasn't in the picture."

"Any boyfriends?"

"The reports mention nothing about a boyfriend."

"Anything about what motive the two would have to run off if they were both enrolled in college and working?"

Martina shook her head. "Nope. I'll put twenty bucks in the jar that they didn't run away."

"I'll get a jar," Vincent joked.

A twenty-year-old case? This would be a doozy. "Let me see the paperwork."

Martina handed me the file, and I read through the names on the reports and statements. The responding officer's name caused me to take a pause. I recognized the last name, and something stirred inside of me. "There's little to go on here. We'll need to interview anyone and everyone who knew or crossed paths with them. Starting with their aunt. It's been twenty years, but if we can learn more about Esther and Loretta, we might have a shot at finding out what happened to them."

"Should we arrange for the media liaison to meet us to put out a press conference — get their pictures in the news?"

I glanced back down at the name. "No, not yet. Let me check something out first."

"Do you have to get the green light from Lafontaine?"

"No. If you run into him, don't mention the case."

"Why?" Vincent asked.

"The responding officer, the person responsible for the missing person case, is familiar. I don't want to unscrew a can of worms if we don't have to."

Martina peered over at the form. "Do you know David Xavier?"

"No, but I know the family name, Xavier. A political family. Let's keep the case between the three of us for now. Can you do that?"

"Of course," Martina said with a winning smile.

"I'm serious."

Martina waved her hand at me. "I'm only teasing. Of course, this case stays between the three of us. What are you thinking?"

"Well, the mayor of San Ramon is Paul Xavier. He's also put

his hat in the ring for governor. I want to find out if David Xavier is connected to the mayor. We don't want to say the original investigator, who may be related to a political family, dropped the ball on a twenty-year-old cold case. We don't want to ruffle too many feathers here. I'm not saying we don't investigate. We will investigate, and we will find these girls. But twenty years ago, things operated differently."

Martina smirked. "Boys' club?"

"On steroids. This is obviously a case of shoddy police work. We don't need to blast to the press that the mayor's relative is problematic — not yet. I don't know if it's a brother or cousin or no relation at all."

Martina nodded.

We had worked a case where we had learned that a set of missing girls had been the work of a serial killer, more notably the son of a retired member of our department who had kept fumbling each of the missing persons cases and not reviewing them at briefing meetings so the connections couldn't be made. It was really ugly, and if we hadn't been able to prove within a reasonable doubt that all involved were guilty, it could have meant the end of the Cold Case Squad.

Vincent said, "I can perform the background. Quietly."

"I appreciate it." After being gone for three weeks to prepare for the wedding and honeymoon, the paperwork and unread emails were practically coming out of my ears. And in the past week, I had barely made a dent.

Vincent said, "All right, boss. I'll get right on it."

"I'll work with Vincent and get the contact information for Loretta and Esther's family. Based on what I've seen, the intake officer wasn't adept at note-taking. Or investigating. We'll sort this out. I'll take the lead for now. I know you have your hands full."

"I appreciate that."

"You want to help us interview or just update you?"

"Let me know when you have them set up and I'll assess. I'd like to be there. I want to make sure we find these two. Their family deserves it. They deserve it."

"You won't get an argument from me."

It was good to be back.

4

LORI

"You're loving this weather, aren't you?" Este teased.

Grinning, I pulled up my sunglasses and said, "You know it. I'm never moving back to the south. The air is crisp and cool. If we were back home, we'd be sweating like pigs right now." It was like year-long springtime. We had only lived in California during the fall, winter, and spring. Locals told us it was hot during the summer months, but it couldn't be Louisiana hot.

Even though we grew up in New Orleans, I didn't miss it, not one bit. It wasn't just the weather. With Mama gone, there was nothing there for me anymore. In California, everything happened so fast. It was the place for movers and shakers. I planned to do it all.

"True, but you sure are showing a lot of skin for March."

"It's 75 degrees out. Look around you. Everyone's in a sundress but you, weirdo."

Este shook her head. "You know, we can go to a club if you want to meet a man."

"I'm not trying to meet a man. I'm simply fitting in. I think I could live here forever."

And maybe I would. Of course, I would not be waiting for

18

some man to provide for me. Our mama taught us better than that. She was a single mother who had raised a set of twin girls. Mama worked two jobs to make sure we never went hungry. We tried not to give her too much trouble, but sometimes Este and I had a problem with that. Nothing serious, just a sip of alcohol or missing curfew from time to time. I regretted those times. Living a life without her made me realize that.

Mama was so kind and funny, but tough too. She worked so much that we did what we could to help, like cooking dinner when she worked late or cleaning up without being asked. Thinking about Mama made me see I would give anything to go back and be with her, but that's not what the Lord wanted. If the Lord that Mama prayed to every night even existed. I still struggled with that concept. If he was there, why would he take her when Este and I needed her so much? Mama's passing left Este and me all alone. Well, other than Aunt Araceli, who offered to let us live with her while we went to college in California.

When she offered, neither Este nor I hesitated. We had little money, but we had Mama's life insurance. With it, we bought a car and drove across the United States to California — the San Francisco Bay Area — and we shared a room in Auntie's house. One day, I hoped to have my own place with Este, but it was a nice house with a nice back yard that had an apple, pear, and even a pomegranate tree. Auntie showed us we could pluck fruit off a tree and eat it right where we stood. No pesticides. It was the same for her vegetable garden. She was teaching us about the soil and plants and what to grow when. Auntie said it was her paradise.

We had only seen Auntie a few times growing up because she lived in California with her husband, who passed right around when Mama did. But she and Mama were close and talked on the phone every single day and, of course, we would say hello too. Auntie didn't have any kids of her own, so I guess without us, Auntie was alone too. Other than Auntie, we didn't have a lot of extended family, but they were a good family, just far away in Honduras. Este and I were lucky, despite being orphans, because we had each other.

We both wanted to make Mama proud. Last fall, when we moved to California, we enrolled at the local junior college. We passed our first semester as pre-med hopefuls and were killing it in our second semester too. We both decided on majoring in biology. I wanted to be a doctor, and Este wanted to be a psychiatrist. Both doctors, but one healed the body, and the other healed the mind. With all As and one B the last semester, I hoped for all As in the spring. Este and I decided to be conservative with the money from Mama's insurance to ensure we could pay for college, so most went to savings and I took a part-time job. Working was fun. I was meeting people each day. The locals were friendly. Maybe it was the neighborhood — living in San Ramon. What could they possibly be upset about?

After I took a sip of my chocolate milkshake, I set it down and watched Este play with her french fries. "What should we do this weekend?"

"The weather is beautiful. We could go for a hike or drive out to the coast again. I admit, I love being near the Pacific Ocean. The cliffs and bridges are so cool."

"Sounds good to me. I work Saturday morning, but I'm free the rest of the weekend."

"It's a date. Have you finished your calculus homework?"

"Not yet. When we get home, I'll..." Before I could give her my update, a young man with dark hair and a smile approached. He had the most dazzling blue eyes I'd ever seen. His smile showed bright white teeth and likely years of braces. He was probably rich. Most folks around town were. I couldn't help but smile back. Standing in front of our table, he said, "Hi, are you two new around here?"

I giggled like an idiot. "This is our second semester. How about you?"

"It's my last semester before I transfer to UC Berkeley."

An older man. An older, intelligent man. "What are you majoring in?"

"Criminal justice. What's your name?"

"My name's Lori and this is my sister, Este."

"Do I detect a Southern accent?" He paused and scratched his chin. "Louisiana?"

How did he know? "That's right. We just moved here last year."

"No kidding. My grandparents are from Louisiana. New Orleans. Whereabouts are you from?"

With that silly grin still stuck on my face, I said, "New Orleans."

"Well, I have to say this was fate."

"I guess so."

"Hey, maybe I could show you around sometime?"

"Okay." I glanced at Este, who was not smiling. I rolled my eyes. Such a kill joy. She acted like one silly man could ruin our futures. It was nonsense. It was just a date. "What did you have in mind?"

"Have you been to Alameda yet?"

"No."

"They have a beach, great food, and an awesome footbridge you walk across and can look out on the entire bay. It's pretty stunning. Have I convinced you yet?"

I bit my lower lip, trying to play coy. "I'm convinced." I pulled a slip of paper from my notebook and scribbled down my phone number with my name. I glanced up and folded it before handing it to him. He accepted it and that grin of his returned.

"All right, Lori. I'll talk to you soon. Have a good day, and it was nice meeting you too, Este."

Este shrugged. "Bye."

After he walked away, I turned toward Este. "What's wrong with you?"

"Seriously?"

"He's cute. And he's smart."

"I don't trust guys like him."

"Like what?"

"Too smooth. I don't get good vibes."

I waved her off. "Live a little, Este."

5

MARTINA

Mrs. Cruz wore sadness like a funeral dress. Classy and put together but obviously hurting on the inside.

"Hello, Mrs. Cruz. My name is Martina Monroe, and this is my partner, Detective August Hirsch, of the CoCo County Sheriff's Department."

"Oh, yes." Her eyes brightened. "You're looking for the girls. I know they didn't run off. Please come on in."

Mrs. Araceli Cruz ushered us into her living room, where she offered seats on her sofa that was covered in plastic. I wished I had considered covering the furnishings when Zoey was young. Or with Barney, who continued to hide his treats under the pillows of the couch. I was always finding some sort of dog treat gunk smashed into the cushions. Maybe it wasn't too late.

"May I offer you some tea or coffee or some water?"

"I would love some peppermint tea, if you have it."

Hirsch said, "I'll have the same."

Mrs. Cruz smiled and hurried out.

I learned over the years that witnesses liked to be useful, like getting us a beverage. But Hirsch and I were full up on caffeine to the point where I was getting jittery, and it was late in the afternoon. I looked up at the fireplace mantle. There were photos of a young Latino couple and the twins, and a few other framed photographs of friends or family I didn't recognize. The end tables had doilies with candy dishes on them. It was how I pictured a grandmother's home. If my mother moved into her own place or with Sarge, would she have doilies on the furniture and photos of Zoey and me and my brothers on the fireplace mantle?

Mrs. Cruz returned and placed a tray with teacups and a teapot atop the coffee table. She poured carefully into each cup, pouring her own last. "Cream and sugar?"

Hirsch said, "I'd love some."

"One lump or two?"

If I knew Hirsch, he'd ask for at least two.

"Two would be great."

Sometimes I worried Hirsch was a sugar addict. I said, "None for me. Thank you."

Mrs. Cruz poured herself a bit of cream and sat in the chair next to us. "So, you're opening up Lori and Este's case. May I ask, and not to sound ungrateful, but why now?"

I looked at Hirsch and then nodded. "The Cold Case Squad was formed two years ago. Since then, we've been reviewing the old cases. As part of that effort, we came across Loretta and Esther's missing persons file. The circumstances got our attention. We are committed to finding them."

"Well, all right. The original officer insisted that they'd run away. Why would they do that? They had their whole lives ahead of them. Both talented students — whip smart. They lived here rent free, and they had a car the two of them shared. Not to mention the inheritance money they had saved for school."

Had anyone checked their financials? "Was their car ever found?"

"No, it never was."

They didn't have many cameras back then. If they had, we could trace their movements the last day they were seen. In some cases, advancement in technology helped us but the lack of it made it difficult to find the missing. "Do you know where they kept their savings account?"

Mrs. Cruz looked up to the right. "Wells Fargo, I think."

"Did you have access to their account?"

"No, they were adults."

Hirsch raised his brows. There was no mention of financial records in the original file. If there was no movement on the account, chances were the girls were no longer with us.

"What can you tell us about the girls?"

"Well, Este and Lori never went anywhere without each other — most of the time. At first, anyway. They were both enrolled at Diablo Valley College and wanted to go off to medical school after graduating from a four-year university. I have no doubt that is exactly what they would've done if somebody hadn't taken them. Lori — that's what she liked to be called, said Loretta was too old fashioned. Este was the same way. Didn't like to be called Esther." She sipped her tea. "Lori had a job working at Bayou. It's a Louisiana-style restaurant owned by a couple of Californians. They hired Lori almost immediately simply because she was from New Orleans and had the accent to really sell the menu. Everything was going great for those two. They'd lived with me for a year, and they were a delight to have around. Both smart and funny, just like their mama."

"You were close with their mother?"

She nodded sadly. "I was. She's my sister. She died right before the girls moved out here. That's why they moved in with me. I offered them a place to stay and to be near family while they went to college. It's hard losing your mother that young." She let out a heavy sigh.

"Do you know if anybody was bothering Lori or Este before they went missing?"

"No, they never mentioned anything, but I noticed that for some months, especially during the summer, Lori seemed to do her own thing. Like I said, usually Lori and Este were together. But then Lori, not only did she have the job, but it seemed like there was something else keeping her busy. They didn't tell me, but I think a boy was calling here."

"So, maybe Lori had a boyfriend?" Hirsch asked.

"Maybe. They didn't tell me, and I didn't want to pry. I didn't want them to think I was trying to replace their mother."

"But they never mentioned a boyfriend?"

"Not exactly. I certainly never met a boy, but I know Este wasn't pleased with Lori being out late at night sometimes. Which is why I hadn't reported the girls missing for two days. There were a few times when Lori went away for the weekend. She said it was with a friend, but I assumed it was a boy."

If Lori had a boyfriend, why wouldn't she say something about it? "Did you ever ask Este about Lori's boyfriend or why she wouldn't bring him around or talk about him?"

"It's a strange thing, really. But no, I didn't ask... I didn't want to pry, and they were still adjusting. They were good girls. I figured they were both technically adults and didn't need somebody checking up on them all the time. I guess I was wrong."

"After they went missing, did anybody come by looking for them? Or call the house looking for them?"

"No, but now that you say that, Lori used to get calls, but after she disappeared, nobody called for her anymore."

That was suspicious, and my gut was saying Lori had a boyfriend, one she didn't bring around. Secret relationships were almost always a recipe for disaster. "Which room did the girls stay in?"

"It was the guest room. It didn't look much different after they moved in, except it had all their stuff in it."

"May we see it?"

"Of course." Mrs. Cruz set down her teacup.

We followed her down the hallway. She opened a door and stepped inside. "Here it is. I must admit there are a few more boxes than when they were here. I don't get too many visitors anymore. All their stuff is still in the closet. I didn't have a reason to move any of it."

"They didn't take anything with them?"

"Not a thing. Not a hairbrush or a toothbrush. Their suitcases are still here, as you can see." She pointed to two blue suitcases at the bottom of the closet.

What teenage girls left everything they owned behind when running off to start a new life? "What about their toiletries? Are they still in the bathroom they had used?"

"Oh, heavens no. But I packed all of their things and put them in a box, in the closet, next to the suitcases. I didn't have the heart to get rid of anything, in case they came back." She lowered her head.

I think Mrs. Cruz, Hirsch, and I knew those girls weren't coming back.

After taking a few minutes to scan the belongings, I saw nothing out of place. "Do you know if Este and Lori kept a calendar or planner for school?"

"Oh, yes." She walked over to the dresser and opened up a drawer. "Yes, they both had planners for school. That's a good point, and you can look and see what classes they took and what teachers they had and any other appointments. Everything is written down. They didn't use computers for that like they do now."

I smiled and started going through the drawers and found them just as she had recollected. Two planners, both embossed with the green and gold Diablo Valley College logo. "Do you mind if we take these?"

"Please take anything you need to help us find out what happened to the twins."

"Do you know if either of them kept a diary?"

"Not that I know of, but you can look through all their things. I didn't see any when I was tidying up in here."

I quickly flipped through the pages but then thought better of it and pulled an evidence bag out of my backpack and place them inside. "Is there anything else you can tell us about the girls that might help us find them?"

Mrs. Cruz cocked her head and stood frozen for a good ten seconds. "The day before they went missing, they were excited about something. Lori said it was a surprise, and she'd tell me the next day. The next day, they were getting ready, and I heard them giggling and taking pictures."

"She never told you the surprise?"

She shook her head.

"And the camera they used to take pictures? Do you have it?"

She nodded and ran out of the room. She returned with a camera and a photo album in her arms. Flushed, she said, "I can't believe I forgot. I had the film developed. There are photos from that night." Mrs. Cruz handed me the album. "The last few pages are from their last day. Take it with you. Return it when you're done. That will tell you all about those girls."

"Thank you, Mrs. Cruz, you've been really helpful."

"I hope you find them."

We collected boxes of evidence before saying our goodbyes.

My heart was heavy as we headed back to Hirsch's vehicle. Within its confines, I said, "I have a bad feeling about this one."

"That makes two of us. We will find them — more likely, their bodies."

"We'll get Vincent on the financials right away."

"Tell him to continue to keep it quiet."

"All right, I'll let Vincent know."

Hirsch nodded, started the car, and began driving back to the station.

"What's up, Martina?" Vincent's glee came through the cell phone line.

"We're just leaving the aunt's house now. We'll need to check financials for both of them. See if there have been any movements. Also, it sounds like Loretta, or Lori, maybe had had a boyfriend but the aunt never saw him. He never came around."

"That is very interesting."

"Why do you say that?"

"I just got a hit on a Jane Doe recovered from the bay twenty years ago. The woman had likely been in the water for a week or two. They found the remains with a few clothing fragments and jewelry on her, but that's not all. It's a female, eighteen to twenty-two years of age, of Hispanic origin, approximately five feet two inches tall, and... pregnant with a sixteen-week-old fetus."

My heart rate sped up. If it was Lori, we may not only have found her remains, but the fetus's DNA could point us to the identity of the boyfriend.

6

MARTINA

After moving the phone away from my mouth, I said, "Vincent has a Jane Doe that matches the description of one of our girls. But get this — the remains include a sixteen-week-old fetus."

Hirsch shook his head. "Already? When did they discover the remains?"

"Twenty years ago."

"If she was in the missing person database, it would have been an easy match. Why wasn't she matched before?"

Shrugging, I said, "Don't know."

"Did they do DNA?"

"I'll ask."

I moved the phone back up to my mouth. "Hey, Vincent, any chance they have DNA?"

"Nope. But I can call over to Alameda County and see what they have."

"Hirsch said it should've been an easy match if she were in the missing persons database. Does it say if a search was done?"

"I'll look into it."

"And I wonder if it makes sense to have them transfer the remains and any evidence to our lab."

"Not a bad idea, especially if we're collecting remains from all over the state. I'll ask."

"Thanks, Vincent."

"Anything else?"

"I need the information for the owners of the Bayou Restaurant in San Ramon, California. I need current information. It's where Lori worked."

"You got it, boss."

I ended the call and put it back in my bag. Hirsch said, "If one of them was pregnant, and we're assuming it's Lori with the secret boyfriend, we could have just found our motive."

"Assuming it's Lori and the boyfriend decided he didn't want a baby or a reminder. But what about Este?"

"The aunt says they were always together. Collateral damage?"

"Or Lori is dead but Este is still out there."

Hirsch's face told me he thought otherwise. "I may have turned into a bit of an optimist with the last few cases, but I think the chances of finding Este or Lori alive are pretty slim. Like almost nonexistent."

I was grateful the girls' aunt had kept all their belongings. We should be able to match DNA from the hairbrush or toothbrush to any remains that we found. "Stranger abduction? It's not out of the question." I made a mental note to tell Vincent to look up any similar disappearances in the area during that time. Records weren't as good going back that far. But if there were a slew of kidnappings or murders in the area, it would be in the newspapers or in the archives. Considering all the cold cases from CoCo County were in our storage closet, we should be able to find that information pretty easily.

Back at the station, we strolled passed Gladys, the receptionist, with a wave. Hirsch said, "You heading home soon?"

"We'll see. I want to go to the forensics lab to talk to Kiki

31

about the case and get her thoughts on testing the remains. I think it's better we speak in person, since we're keeping it under wraps for now."

"Good idea. I'll meet you in the squad room after."

I nodded and headed over to the forensics building. As I walked down the hallway, I approached the sheriff's office and shook my head. Since I had been back from my suspension, I hadn't seen or spoken to the sheriff. He apparently had no desire to talk with me or see me. They gave Hirsch the instruction that all cold case inquiries and updates would go through him and Sarge. No more low-level flunkies like me allowed to grace his office. As if it were a cosmic joke, the sheriff slipped out of his office and gave me a look of death.

Playing it cool, I kept my head held high and continued down the hallway without making a peep. I could feel eyes on me, but I didn't turn around. Instead, I proceeded toward the forensics building and finally arrived at the office of Dr. Katerina Dobbs, or Kiki, as she insisted we call her, the head of the forensics team. I knocked on the door.

"Come in."

"Hey, Kiki. How's it going?"

"I'm doing well, busy as always. What can I help you with?"

After shutting the office door, I sat across from Kiki. "I apologize for the clandestine meeting. Hirsch and I have opened a new case, and there's some sensitivity — possible ties to some figures in the community."

"So, whatever we discuss is for my ears only?" she asked, keenly.

"Exactly." I hadn't worked with Kiki long, but from what I'd seen, she was brilliant and was one of the good ones. You wouldn't know it by the state of her office. Stacks of books and piles of paper filled the small office.

"No problem."

With that, I explained the case and the remains found in Alameda County. "I don't know what the protocol is, but does it make sense to bring those remains here so that we can do the forensics in our own lab?"

She folded her arms and leaned back in her chair. "Interesting case. And yes, I think bringing them here would be a good idea, especially if there is another set of remains we'll need to analyze. But we likely need to go through the Medical Examiner's Office to get the remains. Dr. Scribner typically studies the bodies and collects samples for us. What type of remains are we talking about?"

"The only details we have are what Vincent found in the database. The description could be a match for either Lori or Este. We're assuming Lori had a boyfriend and therefore could have been pregnant."

"You don't have to have a boyfriend to get pregnant."

I smiled. "True, it's just a working theory."

"I admit, I've never identified twins in the forensic lab. They have nearly identical DNA, which makes it difficult to differentiate them. What items do you have to compare the DNA?"

I pulled out the bag with the hairbrushes. "So, how will you determine who's who?" I hadn't realized the complexities of a missing twins' case. Probably because I had hoped that they were still alive. But I was with Hirsch on this one. And I thought that if one of them was gone, they both were.

"By any differences they may have. Usually from medical or dental records. Even twins won't have identical dental profiles."

Another mental note to make sure we got the dental records for both girls.

Kiki tucked her dark hair behind her ear. "I can meet with Dr. Scribner and ask her about the protocol for bringing remains in from another county. She likely has more experience at this than I do."

Dr. Scribner, the county medical examiner, was a stylish woman in her fifties, as opposed to Kiki who couldn't have been older than late thirties to early forties.

"I'd appreciate it. We'll also want her to look at the autopsy reports and the remains. She usually consults for our cold cases. To make sure the original medical examiner didn't miss something."

"Makes sense. Give me the details, and I'll call over to Dr. Scribner and Alameda County if that's what the next step is. I'll keep you posted."

"Thank you." I got up, picked up my backpack, and was about to leave when she stopped me.

"How are things going, Martina? I heard there were some rumblings in the Cold Case Squad, and you and Vincent were suspended."

I left the door shut. "It's going okay. The sheriff hates me, and he likely won't renew my contract for next year, but I'm just taking it one day at a time. Focusing on the case."

"If it's worth anything, I hope they renew your contract. You and Hirsch make a great team, and from what I've seen, the squad has done a lot of good. Few teams can say that."

"I appreciate that, Kiki."

During my two years at the sheriff's department, I had enjoyed working with a first-class team. From the forensics team to the medical examiner to the investigation teams. There was really only one member who felt like a thorn in my side. And unfortunately, he was the man in charge.

7

MARTINA

Watching the sheriff close his door, I was relieved to avoid another run in with him. Thank goodness for small favors. There were more important things to occupy my thoughts than a small man with an even smaller mind. The to-do list for the case continued to grow. Vincent was going to have his hands full with all the records and research we needed to have done to get an insight into what happened to Este and Lori. Not to mention we needed to review all the planners, photos, and personal effects provided by the girls' aunt.

Despite the late hour, the conversation with Kiki re-energized me, and I wanted to dive headfirst into the case. Feeling good, I stepped inside the squad room but quickly slowed my roll. Sarge, also known as my mother's boyfriend, was in the room speaking privately with Hirsch. Of all the people for my mom to date. He was Hirsch's boss, the cold case squad's boss, and the direct line to the sheriff. Sarge was a good guy, but like everyone else on the force, he had to follow orders from the brass, i.e. the sheriff. Things hadn't quite been the same with Sarge since he suspended me. I knew it wasn't his choice, but it had put space between us that hadn't been there before.

Since my suspension, he didn't come by the house as much as before. Mom had been spending more and more time at his place, and they had spent a few weekends away. Was I being paranoid? Maybe they were just progressing in their relationship? Had I become that out of touch with how romantic relationships worked? Probably. Considering I had been on exactly one date in three years, all signs pointed to yes.

I waved before setting my backpack down on the empty chair and took out all the documents we had taken from the twins' room and set them next to the box Hirsch had carried in. If this had been three months ago, I would've walked up to Sarge and maybe gave him a playful punch in the shoulder and asked him how the heck he was. Those days were gone. Some might say it was my fault, considering Vincent and I were the ones who broke the rules. Afterward, I promised Hirsch I wouldn't go rogue again as long as I was at the sheriff's department. And I knew Vincent had learned his lesson. We minded all the p's and q's.

Seated, I flipped open Este Gomez's planner, but before I could start reading, Hirsch and Sarge approached. Sarge cleared his throat. "Hi, Martina. How are you doing?"

"Doing great, Sarge, how about yourself?"

"Doing well. I was just talking to Hirsch about your case."

Hirsch gave me a slight head shake, as if he hadn't given him any details. "Another one to keep us busy."

"I'll be looking forward to an update soon."

"Sure thing."

"You take care now."

"You too."

With that, Sarge left the squad room.

Hirsch grabbed a seat next to me. "I told him we were working on a new case, but I didn't give him any details. I told him I wanted to wait until we had some concrete information to share. But he seems suspicious."

"I got that vibe too."

"What did Kiki say?"

"She's in and will speak with Dr. Scribner about bringing the remains back to our labs. She pointed out something kind of interesting, though. She said twins have nearly identical DNA. The only way we can differentiate them, assuming we find them both, is by medical or dental records."

"Identical DNA. Something tells me this isn't going to be an easy one."

"No, not at all. The next step is to go through their effects while Vincent's doing his research. If your plate is too full, I can take a stab at them. I want to start with the school planners."

"I have time now."

"Great." I pushed a stack of notebooks and papers to Hirsch. "Here's Este's. I'll look through Lori's."

He nodded, and we got to work.

On the inside cover of the school planner, the name Lori Gomez was penned in blue ink across the space, with a smattering of hearts drawn all over the page, along with the usual contact information filled in like a diligent student. Flipping through the calendar, I saw that Lori had listed class times and assignments. Calculus. Biology. Chemistry. English. Sociology. Lori was a busy student. It wasn't until October she started listing her work schedule. That was helpful. But there was no hint of a boyfriend or anything other than school and work through January. Nothing special noted on February 14, Valentine's Day. Did she not go to parties? Or did she just not write them down? Maybe the girls didn't socialize much. Were they having a difficult time adjusting and making friends? It didn't fit with the aunt's description. But if it were true, maybe they had run back to Louisiana. A boyfriend from back home?

At the sight of March's activities, my spine straightened. On March third, there was a heart penned in red ink. A week later, another heart. And the weekend after. And there were more. Had Lori recorded her every meeting with the mystery boyfriend? As I continued to scan the pages, more and more hearts appeared on the calendar, mostly weekends and around her work schedule and school schedule.

The hearts continued until the end of August. Quickly, I scanned the rest of the year before returning to August. The last heart drawn was the last handwritten annotation from Lori Gomez. And it was the last day Araceli Cruz saw Este and Lori alive. My heart racing, I turned to Hirsch, who was on his cell phone. He nodded and got up and walked off.

Maybe he was talking to Kim. Being newlyweds in love and all that. The man was smiling. He was definitely talking to Kim. He had a tell for when he spoke to her or about her. His eyes were sparkly, and there was usually a little pink in his cheeks, and he wore the faintest of smiles. The man was in love. I was jealous. It had been so long since I'd had those types of feelings for anyone, I couldn't remember what it was like. After my disastrous date with a friend of Kim's a few months back, I hadn't pursued dating further. Not that it wasn't on the table; it was more that I would wait until the sparks were flying instead of a random set up.

Hirsch hung up the phone and walked over. "You find something?"

"I sure did. Look at this." I pointed at the planner. "There's a pattern of hearts starting in March and ending on the last day the twins were seen alive."

"So, she had been dating someone, most likely, and had been for about six months and then poof. They're both gone. I sure would like to know the identity of the boyfriend."

My mind processed the information and put two and two

together. "Plenty of time to have a sixteen-week-old fetus. My gosh. Hirsch, the remains Vincent found could absolutely be Lori."

"DNA will tell us for sure."

Hirsch's lack of enthusiasm made me think he was wanted at home. "You about to head out?"

"Yeah, Kim said she's just starting dinner."

I glanced up at the clock on the wall. "Shoot, I need to get going too." It was six o'clock, and Mom had texted me that dinner would be ready at six-thirty. Grateful Mom cooked almost every night, I didn't like to keep her or Zoey waiting.

Vincent rushed into the room. His eyes were wide, and his blond hair stuck out in all directions. No doubt, he'd been working tirelessly all day. It was quintessential Vincent. "I'm glad you're still here. I have to show you something."

"What is it?" Hirsch asked.

"Besides looking for more possible Jane Doe matches, I've started digging into David Xavier, the responding officer. Well, you were right. He's cousins with the current mayor of San Ramon, Paul Xavier. But that's not all. I found multiple news articles with Paul Xavier standing next to another one of our favorite politicians, Sheriff Lafontaine."

We absolutely needed to keep the case under wraps. I didn't trust Lafontaine any further than I could throw him. And I had envisioned throwing him out the window a time or two.

Hirsch looked pensive. "What is the nature of the photos? Campaigning or what?"

"Social events. Campaign events."

They were tight. How tight? Tight enough to cover up a double murder?

Hirsch said, "We keep this very quiet between the three of us and Kiki. Understood?"

"Understood."

Vincent said, "Understood, boss."

But something in Vincent's eyes told me there was a reason we may need to watch our backs. Vincent had good instincts, and he wasn't one to be overly nervous about things. Typically, he kept conversations lighthearted and filled with witty banter. Something told me he feared something, and I wondered what it was and why he hadn't said it in front of Hirsch.

8

LORI

Electricity shot through my fingertips as he placed his warm hand atop mine. The restaurant was dark. The only illumination was the candle flickering on the table, accentuating his bright blue eyes and killer smile. It was the most romantic date I had ever been on, and we had only been to dinner. The Mexican restaurant was a little hole in the wall with decent street tacos and mouth-watering guacamole. But the best part was Freddie. He gave me butterflies from the moment our eyes met. "How do you feel about dessert?" he asked.

"I love dessert."

"Me too. They have great churros. They serve them warm with a scoop of vanilla ice cream with a hint of cinnamon. Should we share one?"

I nodded and grinned like an idiot. He moved his hand off mine and raised it to get the server's attention. A man wearing black trousers and a white button-down shirt rushed over. "We'd like an order of the churros. We're going to share."

The server said, "Excellent choice," and hurried away.

"So, tell me. What was it like growing up in the South? I'm guessing it's quite different from the Bay Area."

"It probably isn't so different. We have a slower pace but still have school and chores and all the usual activities. But this is my first year not celebrating Mardi Gras. It wasn't until recently that I found out not everyone gets time off school to celebrate."

"That's cool. You ever do any voodoo?"

"No, not everyone from New Orleans is a witch doctor."

"Just making sure you don't plan to put a spell on me."

"Well, I can't make any promises."

He chuckled. "Noted. I hear there are a lot of haunted places. Have you ever seen a ghost?"

"A ghost? No."

"Do you believe in ghosts?"

"I do. You?"

"No."

"They say nonbelievers are the ones most likely to be haunted."

He shifted in his seat. "I'll keep that in mind in case you choose to haunt me."

"Again, I can't make any promises that I won't."

He laughed. "Well, we don't have as many Mardi Gras celebrations or haunted houses here. Do you like it anyway?"

"I do. Everything in California seems fast, and everybody's going somewhere in a hurry. But it's clean and green and beautiful. I really like it, especially the weather. I could get used to this."

"You plan to stay in California for a while?"

"I do. I'd like to transfer to a four-year in California." Not that I had plans beyond my four years, but if things went according to plan with Freddie and we were together, I could go to UC Berkeley, too. I could stay with Auntie and save money. I knew it was only the first date, but there was something about Freddie I couldn't shake. Like we were meant to be together.

Maybe it was something in his laugh or the way he said my name. I had never been out with a boy like him before. He was so sure of himself. A man who took charge.

The dessert arrived, and the scent of cinnamon and fried dough was heavenly. At the sight of the two forks, I was ready to dig in but then remembered my manners. I wasn't out with my sister, I was out with a boy. Strike that, a man.

"Come on, let's dig in."

And I giggled as I did. It made me feel like a little kid. Carefree, like everything was unicorns and rainbows. We laughed through dessert that we polished off in about sixty seconds. He said he liked sweets and wasn't kidding.

After Freddie paid the bill, we walked outside, and he said, "Can I show you one of my favorite sites in the city?"

"Where's that?"

"There's a bridge just down the road. You walk across it and can look out at the bay. It's the spot I told you about when we met at school."

"Right. Sounds great."

He grabbed my hand, and the jolts of electricity returned. I had never held hands on a first date before, but then again, I hadn't been on many dates. We walked in silence as we strolled down the street. "Here it is. Come on."

He released my hand and ran to the center of the bridge. Following behind, I tried not to continue giggling like a schoolgirl. He stopped and put his hands on my shoulders and gently turned me toward the bay. "See? What do you think?"

The blue-green water glittered. "It's gorgeous."

"Is it like this in New Orleans?"

"It's similar. This is cool though. Thank you for bringing me here."

He gazed into my eyes. "Thank you for agreeing to come out with me. I've never met a girl like you."

"No?"

He leaned closer. "No, never." His lips touched mine, and my whole body felt like it was on fire. It felt fast, but it felt right. As he kissed me deeper and deeper, all kinds of thoughts whirled in my mind like, would this be the man I married? Feeling silly, I knew it wasn't likely. At eighteen, I was too young, and we had just met. Of course, much later down the road, after I finished medical school and residency, we could get married and have kids. There was plenty of time for that. He released me and said, "You're amazing."

My cheeks were on fire. "You are too."

"Now, how about I show you the beach? It's not the best beach in California, but it's nice, and the sun is about to go down. We can watch the sunset over the water."

I nodded, still in a daze from the kiss.

We held hands as we walked back to his car, where he opened the door for me and shut it after he tucked me in. As he drove, he spoke about his plans for the future.

He seemed to have it all figured out. He parked near the beach and then exited the car and went around back. I met him at the trunk and watched as he pulled out a blanket. He was prepared. My heart fluttered. I couldn't believe he made these plans for me.

With the plaid blanket tucked under his arm, he grabbed my hand, and we ran onto the beach. He straightened out the blanket on the sand and said, "After you."

The wind blew through my hair, blocking my face as I knelt down and seated myself. Cozied up next to one another, Freddie tucked a strand of my unruly hair behind my ear. "Now that's better. I don't want to obscure my view."

I playfully swatted at his arm. "I thought we were here to watch the sunset?"

"It's not as beautiful as my current view."

Embarrassed, I looked away and noticed there weren't many people out. It wasn't too surprising. There was quite a chill in the air as the sun went down. It was colder than San Ramon, being by the water and all. A shiver went through me, and Freddie scooted closer, wrapping his arm around me. "Are you cold?"

"Not anymore." I rested my head on his shoulder as we stared out at the ocean and watched as the sun dipped down and was lost below the sea.

In the darkness, he turned and kissed me gently, pushing me back until I was lying on my back. He climbed on top of me and began kissing me, running his hands down my sides. He whispered, "Lori, I want you so bad."

This was much too fast, especially in a public place. His hand slipped under my jacket. I could feel his cool fingertips on my abdomen, and I pushed him back. "I'm not ready for that."

"Are you sure? I want to be with you so bad."

After straightening my clothes, I sat up. He knelt down and faced me. "I'm so sorry. I'm moving too fast. I just really like you. You're so beautiful."

"It was moving a little fast. I'm only comfortable kissing. Is that okay?"

"Of course. I totally respect you and your decision. We can go as slow as you want."

"You're amazing."

"No, you are."

It knew it was ridiculous, but I swear at that moment, I fell in love with him.

9

HIRSCH

Vincent had a hunch and ran with it. His gut feeling turned out to be correct, leading me to be sitting in my car outside the sheriff's department contemplating how we would move forward on the Gomez sisters' case.

Vincent had discovered a deep connection between Xavier and Lafontaine. They were close, not just political allies. They went to high school together and then to college. Besties, as the kids say. With that information, it meant we had to tread carefully with the case until I could prove Xavier's cousin wasn't involved in a cover-up or terrible policing regarding Lori and Este's disappearance. The probability was low that they had taken part in any wrongdoing, but if that turned out to be a bad assumption and they were involved, it would halt the investigation. No answers. No justice. No finding Lori and Este.

When Sarge had asked about our case, I'd explained it would be a big one, but we were waiting on some background and didn't want to say anything too prematurely. Sarge seemed curious about the whole thing. That was two days earlier, and I had yet to provide an update. I could only stay silent for so long.

Surely when someone tells you nothing about a case, you want to know everything about that case. Sarge was a good man and a good boss, and he was good police. How long could we keep it quiet?

The Cold Case Squad had continued to exist mostly because of the good publicity we had brought Sheriff Lafontaine. We needed to keep bringing that, not disparaging his buddy's good name. Maybe I could urge the other members of the squad to take on a really high-profile case to get the heat off us. Share the limelight. They were more than capable. But somehow Martina had this way of picking the biggest, most outrageous cases. She said it was a gift. Like her, I didn't shy away from challenges, but we had come dangerously close to losing the entire squad, and I wouldn't let that happen again.

When the Cold Case Squad was formed, I thought it would be a lower stress job than working homicide. In some ways, it was, with the slower pace and the ability for most of the team to work fairly regular hours. But I hadn't factored in the stress of being the squad leader. The tough conversations and politics and piles of paperwork were eating away at me. My only true breaks over the last two years were when I was home with Kim and during the honeymoon. I had questioned if the job was right for Kim and our family. Going back to homicide wasn't a good option, considering that would take me out of the house at all hours of the day and night. The other option seemed unfathomable, but I couldn't ignore it.

My twenty years on the force were coming up, and I had the option to retire with a pension. Between the pension and a part-time gig in security or PI work, we could have a good life where I wouldn't miss out on the important things. There was so much to think about. I wasn't used to having more than myself to think of, but with Kim and discussions about our future... I wondered what it would look like. Could I sustain my current career choice?

My phone buzzed. Martina calling me back. Ignoring the call, considering we'd be face-to-face in just a few minutes, I stepped out of my car. It was time to face the music.

It was decided.

Sarge had to be brought in on the investigation. If that meant he would shut it down, so be it. I couldn't only think of Martina and my desire to solve the case. There were too many other people to consider.

I locked the car door and started toward the entrance, wearing my best happy face. Never let them see you sweat.

Strolling through the lobby, I said, "Good morning."

Gladys smiled widely. "Good morning, Detective Hirsch."

"How have you been?"

"Life's treating me pretty good. How's that new wife of yours?"

"She's like sunshine."

"I swear if I'd found one of you back in my day, I'd be singing and dancing all day long."

I didn't really know what that meant, but I thought she intended it as a compliment. "Have a good one."

"You too."

Yes, I was madly in love with my wife, and I was one lucky man to have found her. I had nearly given up on love and was hesitant when Betty, Martina's mother, had set me up with her bingo friend's daughter, but I fell in love with Kim almost instantly. She was the brightest spot in my day, every day since I met her.

At Sarge's office, I poked my head in. He was an early bird like me and had the look of thirty-five years on the force in his eyes. "Hey, Sarge. You got a minute?"

His face fell. "Sure, close the door."

I shut the door behind me and took the seat in front of Sarge. "I wanted to talk to you about Martina and my new case."

He set down his pen. "I'm listening."

"Missing eighteen-year-old sisters — twins. Disappeared twenty years ago from San Ramon. There's barely any ink on the reports. No investigations were done. Simply labeled runaways. Although the two girls were students at the local junior college with plans for medical school. They just moved here a year before from Louisiana and were living with their aunt. One had a job. We think one had a boyfriend, but nobody seemed to know his name."

"Okay, sounds like a good case to reopen. I don't remember hearing anything about it. But I was working in Alameda County back then. But still. Twins?"

"The girls are Hispanic. There were no headlines. Barely an investigation. Based on a planner kept by one girl, we think she had a date the last night the two were seen alive."

Sarge squinted, as if waiting for the punchline. "Sounds like an excellent case. What's the issue?"

"Well, that's why I'm here. It's sensitive. Which is why we have kept the details quiet — out of extreme caution for optics."

Sarge laughed sarcastically. "Extreme caution for optics? Oh boy, let me have it."

He knew it was going to be bad. I said, "The person who took the report for the missing sisters was David Xavier. He's the cousin of Paul Xavier, the mayor of San Ramon and gubernatorial candidate."

"And you're wondering if you point out the piss-poor investigation, it will make the mayor look bad?"

"Yes, but that's not all. Paul Xavier and Sheriff Lafontaine are old high school and college buddies. Good friends, like brothers."

Sarge let out a low whistle. "Boy, do you know how to step in it?"

"You see why we've been exercising caution. I'm bringing it to you because I really want to solve this case, and I think we can do it. It won't be an easy shot, but those girls deserve to be found. But if Xavier and his cousin were close, it could come back at us — through Lafontaine. You and I both know the Cold Case Squad can't take any more lashings from him."

Sarge crossed his arms. He glanced over at the wall, as if contemplating what kind of advice to give me. We sat there in silence for a minute, maybe two. Sarge was a careful man. "The team is currently working on several cases, right?"

"That's right."

He nodded. "Here's what we're going to do. On paper, you'll take over one case in-progress. You'll have to have a conversation with whoever you take it from, but you're not really taking it. We keep the Gomez sisters' case quiet until we can rule out any sort of wrongdoing by the Xavier family, okay?"

"All right. Anything else?"

"Actually, yes. Help a little on the other case, so that it's not a bald-faced lie."

"Thank you, Sarge."

"Those girls deserved better back then. It's time to right that wrong. And something tells me that if your team is cautious, they have good reason to be. Now, go and do what you do best. I'll take care of the sheriff."

With that, I felt my body relax just a smidgen and made my way to the squad room. Before I could reach the door, Vincent was by my side. "Hey, Hirsch."

His clothes were wrinkled, and his hair was all over the place. "Did you go home last night?"

He shook his head. "No, but I think we found another potential match. There's actually a few. I flagged three."

"Three sets of remains that could be one of our sisters?"

"There is one I think is most likely her — but there are two others I didn't want to rule out without Dr. Scribner's and Kiki's input."

If we could find the remains, it would be useful in determining what happened to the girls. My gut said they were dead. But I wanted to know how they got that way. "Good. You talk to Martina?"

"Not yet."

"I'll let her know when she comes in. She's been working with Kiki and Dr. Scribner. How's the rest of the research going?"

"I found their bank accounts. No movement since they went missing. And I have contact information for the owners of the restaurant where Lori worked. I left three messages and haven't gotten a call back. I'll keep trying."

No movement in their bank account in twenty years. I knew what that meant. There was no way Lori and Este ran away. "Good work. Why don't you go home and get some rest?"

"Nah. I'll be all right. I'm still young," he said with a smirk.

I couldn't argue with him about that. "All right then, I'll see you for the morning meeting."

He nodded and rushed off.

As I entered the room, I saw that some squad members had already arrived. Wolf and Jayda were talking animatedly. The team was working on two cases. One of their cases would be a good option for us to shadow and take credit for. It wasn't cool to take credit for their work, but I thought they'd understand. I waved.

"Hey, Hirsch."

"I need to talk to you about something."

Their faces grew worried. Clearly, I needed to work on my reputation. Jayda said, "Sure thing."

"It's nothing bad..." And I explained the situation. We were running a covert operation. It was ridiculous we had to act in such a way in order to bring justice for two missing sisters. Part of me didn't feel right about it, but the other part knew it was the only way.

10

MARTINA

Excitement filled my veins as Hirsch and I strolled toward the autopsy suite. We were meeting with Kiki and Dr. Scribner to discuss the four sets of remains that three different counties had sent over. From what I'd learned, we were lucky the remains had yet to be buried and were still in storage. There were quite a few Jane Does in California but only a few who matched the Gomez sisters. I said a brief prayer that two of those four sets of remains belonged to Lori and Este. Not that I wanted them to be dead, but I wanted them to be found. And whoever took their lives needed to be held accountable.

We reached the suite and as we gowned up, I realized how valuable the relationships we had built with the medical examiner, Dr. Scribner, and the head of the forensic lab, Dr. Kiki, Dobbs were. They were willing to work with us under the radar to help us find the Gomez sisters. Nobody deserved to be missing.

Dr. Scribner and Kiki were good people. I had seen it from the first time I met each of them. They both were in this job for the same reason Hirsch and I were. Not for the money or for the glory, but to bring the missing home and to solve crimes to give the families answers. I knew firsthand not knowing was far worse than knowing. We wanted to provide answers for families, and we chose murders and missing persons, but the head of the forensic lab did more than just that. The forensics and crime scene team helped solve home invasions, burglaries, and other types of crimes that we didn't touch. One time, Kiki explained those cases were important too because everybody deserved answers and that when you're robbed or someone breaks into your home, your sense of security evaporates. By catching the perpetrators, she's able to return a bit of the victim's security back.

"You ready?" Hirsch asked behind his face mask.

"That I am, detective."

We pushed through to the suite, and my eyes drifted to the four metal tables, each with a set of skeletal remains laid out. Dr. Scribner said, "Hello, Ms. Monroe and Detective Hirsch. Good to see the two of you."

"You too."

It had been a while since we worked with Dr. Scribner. One of the most intelligent women I'd ever met, and she was standing next to the second. Dr. Katerina Dobbs. She was newer to us, but she impressed me from here to the core of the earth. "Hi, Kiki."

"Good to see you two."

"So, what do you have for us?" Hirsch asked.

Dr. Scribner walked us to the first table, displaying two bodies. One was an adult about five feet tall with long dark hair, and the other was the tiniest skeleton I'd ever seen. At the end of the table were evidence bags. Dr. Scribner said, "We received Jane Doe One and Baby Doe from Alameda County. Along with the bones, they sent the forensic evidence collected from her body — clothing, jewelry, and fingernail clippings. They also sent tissue samples."

Hirsch said, "The baby. What can you tell us?"

She nodded. "Sixteen weeks. Male."

I looked over at Kiki. "Do we have enough to get DNA for the mother and father?"

"Absolutely. Whoever killed this mother and child made a mistake by throwing them in the water. She was well preserved when she was found. Alameda County did a good job of collecting evidence and storing it properly."

Thank goodness.

Kiki continued over to the stack of evidence bags. "I reviewed the evidence and the original autopsy photos with Dr. Scribner. All the evidence was photographed. Like I said, Alameda County did a good job. Come here, I have the photos." She grabbed a stack of items near the evidence bags and set down each of the photographs.

Huddled around, I studied the post-mortem photos.

"They took these before the autopsy. It is how she was found."

Her skin was discolored and bloated, but even I could see the resemblance to Lori and Este. I flinched at the photo of the fetus. We had to find the monster who did this. "She looks like the girls."

Dr. Scribner said, "That's what I thought too."

Kiki said, "The clothing will help us if there's any blood or other fluids, but she had been in the water, so it's unlikely we'll get anything useful from her clothing remnants. But we'll be able to get DNA from the tissue samples."

"Cause of death?" Hirsch asked.

"She had several broken bones, but the original ME concluded based on the condition of the brain and other organs, she drowned. He concluded she likely had sustained a fall prior — likely off a bridge or tumble from a cliff causing the damage to her bones, which may have incapacitated her, leading to the drowning."

Hirsch and I continued to study the pictures. Sickened that a young life had become gruesome photos.

"When you're ready, we can go over to Jane Does two, three, and four."

Four Jane Does.

Terrible.

Hirsch and I exchanged glances and moved to the next table. Dr. Scribner said, "Jane Doe Two was found just a few years ago. She'd been buried for at least twenty years. All that remained were hair and bones. Same age range, build, and of Hispanic origin. The difference is this person has never given birth and they're approximately 5'4" tall. Whereas One was approximately 5'2"."

"Este and Lori's driver's licenses state they were 5'2"."

"Correct."

"Where was she found?" Hirsch asked.

"The paperwork said Oakland Hills."

"So, also from Alameda County?"

"Yes."

"All we have are the remains and a few clothing fragments. DNA will be trickier, but hopefully we'll be able to get a usable sample," Kiki said before walking to the end of the table and pulling out photos of Jane Doe Two. They were similar to what lay on the table. Shaking my head, I hated that the woman didn't have a name, but I was sure it wasn't Lori or Este. Wrong height.

Dr. Scribner said, "Two's cause of death is likely strangulation because of a broken hyoid bone. I don't think she's one of our girls. Let's look at Three."

We followed her and Kiki. "If I had to guess, I'd say based

on the brow ridges, cheeks, the nose, chin, overall structure of the skeleton, minus fetus, she's One's twin."

Staring down at the skeleton, my heart raced. "Seriously?"

She nodded. "If they weren't identical twins, the similarity between the two skeletons wouldn't be so striking. It's not definitive, but it makes me hopeful."

Kiki added, "DNA will confirm if they are twins."

"Where did she come from?"

"Calaveras County. She was unearthed five years ago. Cause of death was exsanguination — loss of blood because of sixteen stab wounds to the chest. But based on the photos, I think it was the second attempt at killing her."

Moving to the end of the table, Kiki laid out the photos. Dr. Scribner explained, "See here? There is a red scarf wrapped around her neck. We think the perp tried to strangle her, but it took too long, and he improvised."

Hirsch said, "The perp was likely inexperienced."

"Exactly. So when it took too long, he pulled out a knife and stabbed her repeatedly in the chest and neck. The knife was small, likely a pocketknife or similar. The killer was messy. You can see there's a lot of blood on her clothing."

A lightbulb turned on. "If he was inexperienced, his hand likely slipped on the blood, cutting himself."

Kiki said, "Exactly what we're hoping for. If he cut himself, he left his DNA behind."

Hirsch said, "Fingers crossed."

We moved down to the fourth and final table with the remains of Jane Doe Four. "As you can see, the skeleton is very similar to Two. The only difference is she's a bit taller at about 5'6".

"Not Lori or Este."

"No, not likely." Dr. Scribner removed her glasses and let

them hang on the beaded string. "You two bring me the most interesting cases."

This was amazing news.

Vincent said he was fairly certain he'd found our sisters. How had he found them so quickly? Despite him explaining that he put in specific parameters of the sisters' height, weight, age, and race, I had doubted it, thinking it would be more like a needle in a haystack. "Wow."

Hirsch said, "My thoughts exactly. So, what do we do next?"

"Based on our observations, the most likely outcome is that our sisters are One and Three. Kiki and I discussed working together to make our final assessments and process the forensics. Kiki will start with DNA testing on One, Three, and Baby Doe."

Kiki added, "Unfortunately, the DNA can take up to a week. But I'm hoping it will go faster because I'll start with One and Three, running their DNA side-by-side. They should be nearly identical, so we can identify if they're twins first and then determine if they are the Gomez twins. If they are, we'll move on to Baby Doe's DNA and start testing the evidence found on Three."

"Is there anything else you need from us?" I asked.

"Have you requested medical and dental records yet?" Dr. Scribner asked.

"Vincent requested them earlier today."

"That'll be important to identify who's who. Were they local?"

"The girls grew up in Louisiana."

Dr. Scribner frowned. "Twenty-year-old records from Louisiana. Good luck."

I didn't like the sound of that. "Thanks."

"If you have any questions, come to one of us directly. We won't be sharing the case with our teams," Kiki added.

Hirsch said, "Many thanks to my two favorite scientists."

Based on the crinkles near their eyes, I could tell that got a smile out of Kiki and Dr. Scribner. "I second that. We'll let you get to it. Thank you both again. Sincerely."

"It's why we do this job."

We said our goodbyes and removed our PPE while I prayed we could identify Lori and Este.

11

MARTINA

Nodding, I said, "That is a pretty interesting case. How far have you gotten on it?"

Jayda said, "We've reviewed the forensic evidence with Kiki, and they're reprocessing some items. It's in the queue to be processed, but apparently there's a backlog like usual."

I had a feeling I knew where that backlog was coming from. I mean, not that the forensics lab wasn't always busy, but with Kiki dedicated to trying to identify the missing twin sisters, they were down an analyst. "Forensic testing wasn't done ten years ago?"

"They did some. They assumed all the blood on his clothing was from his stab wounds, so they took fingerprints, but no trace or physical evidence was tested. I wouldn't have assumed that, but hey, I wasn't here ten years ago."

Sounded like sloppy police work to me. "It sounds like forensics is taken care of. What can or should I do to help?"

"You could pound the pavement around the park where he was killed. Re-interview neighbors and people who frequented the park."

That was likely a good bet. From what Jayda and Ross

explained to me, the case we would be "helping" with was a ten-year-old unsolved murder. A man by the name of Richard Whitlock, aged thirty-five, had been killed in a neighborhood park in the city of Dublin. The original reports said that it looked like a robbery, but it didn't add up for me or Jayda and Ross. They stabbed Whitlock late at night, approximately eleven pm. That told me he was meeting someone, not out for a casual romp at a park by himself.

"We'll canvas the area. What about financials? Obviously, he was meeting somebody and it went wrong."

"We got that too. We haven't gotten that far. But we should request them. They're not in the file. It's lucky that you and Hirsch have some time now."

Unfortunately, we had a bit more time than I would prefer. It had been almost a week, and we hadn't heard on the DNA results for Jane Does One and Three. My gut was telling me we had found the Gomez sisters. But the circumstances around their deaths were strange. What had happened that night? One of them had drowned in the bay and the other one was found several hours away in Calaveras County, buried in a shallow grave. Why would a killer do that? So they couldn't be connected? But if they were inexperienced as we suspected, maybe they panicked and realized they needed to get away from the first crime scene.

Hirsch walked up. "What's up?"

"I was just talking to them about the Richard Whitlock case. I was telling them we can interview folks around the park where he was killed." No problem. The city of Dublin was next to San Ramon where we had some Gomez sisters business to take care of.

"Yeah, we could do that. We're heading over there anyway, right?" Hirsch asked.

"That's right, and then we should definitely request the

financial and employment records, anything that could point to a motive for this man's murder."

Ross said, "Agreed. We just have our hands tied up right now. We appreciate any help you can give us."

"You got it."

Ross stood up. "All right, we gotta go check out that hot tip on the Daniels case."

Hirsch said, "Good luck out there."

They waved and hurried off. "Any word from Kiki yet?" Hirsch asked.

"Nope."

"Well, at least Jayda and Ross's case is in Dublin, which is right next door to San Ramon. We need to pick up that photo album from Mrs. Cruz."

After reviewing the possessions we had taken from the girls' room, including the photo album Mrs. Cruz had thought their last photos were in, in fact, it didn't contain them. They were photos of them as little girls. She had accidentally mixed up the two. "Since we still haven't been able to get ahold of the owners of the Bayou Restaurant where Lori worked, I thought maybe the surrounding restaurants might remember Lori if they were around back then."

"Let's do it."

I grabbed my backpack, slung it over my shoulder, and headed for the door. Hirsch followed behind. With my hand on the knob, I turned it but felt resistance. Peeking through the tiny window, I smiled. "It's Kiki."

I opened the door and ushered Kiki inside and over to the corner. "Did you get the results yet?"

"Jane Does One and Three are a match. They're identical twins. And I ran DNA from some of the hair follicles from the brush that you submitted. It's a match. We found the Gomez sisters."

I was about to ask follow-up questions when we heard footsteps approaching. Hirsch and I stiffened and turned, but it was Vincent. Vincent hurried over. "What's up?"

"We found the Gomez sisters. It's a match."

"I knew it was them. The one found in the bay and the one found buried in Calaveras County, right?"

"That's right."

Vincent said, "All the stats were there. Height, approximate weight, age, and Hispanic, missing twenty years. They're the only ones it could be."

"Then why give us four?"

He shrugged. "We don't want to be biased. Plus, there weren't that many other Jane Does. I figured maybe once we solved this case, we'd have our next two picked out."

Sneaky. And he had a lot of faith we would close this case quickly.

"What's next?" Vincent asked.

Kiki said, "I'll start working on getting the DNA from the baby and see if we can get a match for the father from CODIS, and then we'll start going through all the materials found on Three. That will take some time because I have to be meticulous. I don't want to miss anything. If there's a drop of the killer's blood on the sister's scarf or blouse, I want to make sure it's analyzed and we get DNA from it."

"Understood." Although patience was not one of my strong suits, I was getting better at it. Plus, we still had so many people to talk to. Surrounding businesses around the restaurant where Lori worked, plus students, administrators, professors, and anybody else who might remember the twins. Between finishing up those interviews, we had the Whitlock case to work on. It would be a lot, but it was better than sitting around waiting for lab results.

12

LORI

Waiting for Freddie at the corner near my house on a sunny afternoon, I reminisced about Freddie and my first month together. After our first date, I knew he would stay with me until the day I died. I mean, the very next day after our first date, he called to ask me for a second date and then a third and a fourth. No games. No wondering when he would call. My whole being screamed he was the one.

Freddie told me he wanted to do something special for our one-month-dating anniversary. I thought that was kind of silly, but it was sweet too. I had never been with a boy like Freddie. A man who wanted me every moment. He didn't like it when I told him I couldn't meet him because I had work or school or needed to study. But eventually he understood that as much as I enjoyed our time together, I had to focus on school too, and I needed to work at the restaurant to have money. It took a while for him to get it. I figured it was because he had been raised in a wealthy family and didn't have to work. I had learned so much about him, like for one, he was older than I thought. He was twenty-two and had taken time off after high school to travel through Europe. And had spent three years in junior college figuring out what he wanted to study. I could only imagine what that kind of luxury would be like.

His silver Honda Civic pulled up, and I waved and greeted him with a giant smile as I climbed into the passenger seat. I leaned over for a kiss, and we embraced momentarily before he continued back on the road. "I'm dying to know where we're going."

"You don't like surprises?"

"No, I do. I'm just really curious."

"I told you it would be special. I had to do some digging to find the perfect thing because you're so special to me."

Swoon. Sometimes I wondered if Freddie was too good to be true and maybe he was. But whatever it was he had done, I'd fallen super hard. I should have known it was going to happen considering the first time he gazed down at me with those ocean blue eyes, I felt weak in the knees.

In the last month, we had seen each other at least twice a week. It was sometimes hard to fit in our time together. But we managed. Sometimes we met for lunch or on the weekend. He didn't have a job, but he had school, and he said he also had a lot of family obligations. Apparently, his family was very important and heavily into state politics. I didn't really understand how that took up so much of his time, but it did. But I let it go. All families were different and had their own set of expectations, and Freddie's was no exception. As much as I didn't understand his world but was intrigued by it, he was shocked at mine. Growing up with a single mother, I only had my sister to keep me company most days and nights. We didn't have a lot of money like his family did. I thought we were a case of opposites attracting. Two poles of a heavy-duty magnet, with nothing capable of stopping the attraction. He held my hand as he drove down the highway. He was heading south, and I had no idea where he was going. "Not even a little hint?"

"Okay, I'll give you a little hint. There is a picnic involved."

Romantic. He continued on I-680 a few miles past Pleasanton, he exited the freeway. The brown sign on the side of the road made me suspect we were going hiking in the Sunol Wilderness. I had never been there, but I read about it, and the trails were supposed to be pretty good, with especially splendid views of what they'd named Little Yosemite.

Este and I had planned to visit one day, but between school and work and Freddie, when I finally had a moment off, I didn't want to hike. Instead, we would sit and watch TV or just gab about Freddie or next semester's classes. Who knew boyfriends took up so much time?

Parked in the visitors' parking, there were only a few more hours of daylight. I didn't see any other cars around. "Are you sure the trails are open?"

"They're open. It's not very busy during the weekdays. I didn't plan our anniversary to be on a weekday, but that's how it turned out, and boy, am I glad it did. We'll practically have the place to ourselves."

He gazed into my eyes, and I gave him a quick peck. I couldn't remember the last time I was this happy. It wasn't all because of Freddie, but he was a big part of it.

Outside, I met him at the trunk where he was pulling out a picnic blanket, paper bag, and a cooler hopefully filled with food because I hadn't eaten since breakfast. "Wow, you really went all out."

"Nothing but the best for you, babe."

I loved the way he called me babe or his girl. I'd never been someone's girl before, and I liked it. Even if it was a little antiquated and probably sexist, but something about when the words came from his lips made it okay. "Can I help?"

"Nope. Just follow me."

I took in the surroundings. It was mostly brown, but there

was a red barn labeled as the visitor center with picnic tables, and I could see a small bridge that looked like it headed back to the hiking trails. Sure enough, there were trail signs. I looked down at my ballet flats and realized I was quite unprepared for a hike. "How far are we hiking?"

"Not far."

We continued past the trail signs and onto a gravel road. "There are some secluded picnic tables up ahead."

"That sounds great." As promised, we soon reached a picnic table that was to his liking.

He set the blanket and bag on top of the table and pulled out a box and a bottle of champagne with two plastic cups. Not of age yet, I wasn't much of a drinker, just sips here and there. Lots of people my age drank, but I wasn't one of those cool kids who went to a lot of parties. Maybe if I had been a cool kid, I would have had more of a taste for it. But tonight was a special occasion, so I planned to embrace the moment and the champagne.

He smoothed out the blanket on the bench and said, "For you." And then he sat next to me. He opened up the cooler, and there was cheese and crackers and little sandwiches. Yummy. There was another small box filled with cookies and cupcakes. A sweet tooth was something we had in common. "This is wonderful. Thank you so much."

He smiled and handed me napkins, then popped open the champagne bottle. As he poured the bubbly into the plastic cups, I thought I was the luckiest girl in the world. He handed me a cup and raised his. "To you and me."

"To you and me."

We clanked our plastic cups together. I took a sip. It was bitter and fizzy. The taste wasn't great, but I kind of liked the bubbles. The cheese and crackers hit the spot. Content, I snuck a cookie and savored the chocolaty goodness. Freddie finished chewing and took my hands into his. Gazing into my eyes, he said, "This has been the best month of my life. There's something I want to tell you."

My heart was nearly beating out of my chest. Was he about to say...

"I love you."

He said it. Feeling tingly all over, I replied, "I love you too."

He grinned and grabbed me for the longest and deepest kiss we had ever shared. Soon we progressed into other things and his hand was way up my shirt and his lips on my neck.

"Hey, let's slow down. We're in a park."

"I love you so much. I want all of you."

"Not here."

He sat up. "You're right. It should be special. I'll take you away for the weekend. We can go to my parents' cabin. It will be amazing, I promise."

"Okay." Was I really ready to lose my virginity?

"It's a date." He finished his cup of champagne and poured himself another full cup.

"You know, I love hearing stories about your friends and your family. When will I get to meet them?"

His smile faded. "Not yet. There is a lot going on right now, plus..." He hesitated, and then his smile returned. "I love that it's just the two of us right now. It's like we're in our own little love bubble."

"I do like our love bubble," I said with a smile.

Having never been in a serious relationship, I guessed that made sense, and I did like that it was just the two of us baring our souls and embracing one another. There was no need to rush it and have other people coming into our relationship sooner than it needed to be.

Once darkness fell, we left the park, and he dropped me off in front of my house and drove off.

Practically floating, I strolled up the steps, but before I could even pull out my key to open the door, it flung open. Este stood there with her hand on her hip. "He can't even walk you to the door?"

I rolled my eyes. "It's not 1950, Este. I'm fine."

"If you say so. How was your night?"

I said, "It was magical," as I twirled around, basking in the love I had in my life.

"Oh yeah? Have you met his friends yet?"

Frowning, I said, "Not yet. We're going to stay in our own little love bubble for a while." Este had known I was getting antsy about not having met his friends or family yet, or vice versa.

"Was that your idea or his?"

"Quiet, Auntie will hear."

Este rolled her eyes.

"You need to chill out."

She shook her head. "Be careful. I don't trust him. It's not right that he doesn't pick you up at the door or pick you up at the house most of the time. Something is off there."

I waved her off. "You don't have to worry about me, sis."

"Mark my words, Lori. You're messing with fire."

13

HIRSCH

It was incredible how quickly we had located the bodies of Este and Lori, but something didn't sit right with me. How had we found them so fast? Why hadn't anyone identified their remains? More upsetting was the manner of their deaths. Who would kill the sisters? What had driven their killer to that? On the job, I had seen firsthand that humans had no limit on how low they could go. How depraved they could be. It made it difficult to trust others, especially strangers. But once trust had been earned, I wouldn't hesitate to go to battle for that person. And I trusted Kiki and Dr. Scribner and Martina, mostly. She was my best friend, but she had done some questionable things. Of course, her heart was in the right place. It always was, and she swore she wouldn't do anything like that again. I had to believe it was true.

Kiki continued, "Dr. Scribner says if you want to come by to discuss any details about Lori and Este's deaths before you notify the family, she's available."

Death notifications were the worst part of the job. "Thank you. We'll head over there now."

Martina said, "We'll walk with you."

We followed Kiki down the hall in silence, considering we knew better than to talk about the case in the event there were unauthorized ears listening. Sure enough, as we approached the sheriff's office, he was just stepping out into the hall. "Detective Hirsch. How are you?"

He studied Martina from head to toe but didn't say a word. He ignored Kiki and returned his attention to me.

"Doing well, sir, how are you?"

"I can't complain. How's the Richard Whitlock case going?"

Thankfully, we had worked out the details with Jayda and Ross, but I was a little surprised Sarge had already spoken to the sheriff about it. "Good. We have most of the forensic evidence awaiting testing at the lab, and we'll be pulling financials, too. It's a start."

"Sounds like it'll be a tough one to solve. But if anybody can do it, you can, Detective Hirsch."

The fact he omitted my partner, Martina, was not lost on me.

"All right, then. I'll leave you to it." The sheriff continued down the hall as the three of us continued in the other direction.

Once out of earshot, Martina let out a deep breath. "That was fun."

Kiki said, "You weren't kidding. He acted like you didn't exist."

"He wishes. And hey, quick thinking on your feet, Hirsch."

"Good thing you briefed me on the case this morning. If you hadn't, I'd be toast." Worry filled my gut. How or why did the sheriff think the Whitlock case would be difficult to solve? How much did he know and, more importantly, why did he care? Oh, jeez. Was all the secrecy making me too suspicious?

"Seriously. You could've blown our cover."

"Yeah, all this covert stuff is making me paranoid."

"Nah. Think of it as a new skill. You can add undercover work to your resume."

Only Martina could turn this into something positive. Not that I disagreed with the approach. I was the one who pushed for it. But something about the look in Martina's eyes told me she enjoyed it.

We arrived at the Medical Examiner's Office and knocked on Dr. Scribner's door. She glanced over her spectacles and said, "Hey. Incredible news, right?"

"I'll say."

"C'mon in."

The three of us milled inside. I said, "Don't worry. We won't take up too much time. The cause of death and manner of death were pretty obvious. Drowning, stabbing. Both homicide."

Dr. Scribner said, "Correct."

"We will do the death notification today. Is there anything else you can tell us? Were the girls sexually assaulted?"

Dr. Scribner said, "Not that we know of. Kiki's testing will confirm or rule it out. There was no obvious sign. I took another look at the reports and photos. I'm pretty certain the pregnant sister was pushed or fell into the water and drowned. Maybe from a bridge. They took the second sister somewhere, strangled, and ultimately stabbed her to death before burying her. I still haven't received the medical or dental records, so I can't say which sister is which."

"Thank you, Dr. Scribner."

Kiki said, "Now we wait for the DNA results on the baby. Hopefully, there's a hit on the father's DNA in CODIS."

Yes, a suspect would be nice. Kiki had warned us it could take over a week to find a match for the father's DNA. That was the next step in the covert operation, as Martina put it. We said our goodbyes to Dr. Scribner and Kiki before heading back down the hall.

"Are you ready to go to Mrs. Cruz's for the death notification?" I asked.

"I'm never ready."

———

ONCE AGAIN SITTING in Mrs. Cruz's living room, I accepted her offer of coffee. I was tired and the news of the day was sucking my energy. Usually, Martina was quite skilled in this area, so I let her take the lead on most notifications. She had a way with the victims' families. Not that I was terrible at it, but she had a warmth and a sympathetic way of consoling them and being sensitive to their news. We had called ahead earlier in the day to pick up the missing photo album, so we were expected. The news that we had found Lori and Este's remains wouldn't be.

Martina started, "Mrs. Cruz. We have a development in the case."

"Oh?"

"We found Lori and Este's remains."

"I knew they hadn't run off." She began to cry, and Martina stood up, went over to the chair in which Mrs. Cruz sat, and put her arm around her shoulder.

"I'm very sorry for your loss, Mrs. Cruz."

Mrs. Cruz wiped her eyes and patted Martina's hand. "You're a good one, aren't you?"

I smiled at that. It was true. Martina was definitely a good one. Mrs. Cruz looked up at me. "Do you know what happened to them?"

We explained to her what we had learned about the sisters' deaths.

"Murdered. I can't imagine who would want to hurt those two girls."

"Mrs. Cruz, one of the girls was pregnant."

Her eyes widened. "How far along?"

"About four months."

"I'm surprised, but if one of them was, it must've been Lori. I suspected she was seeing someone. Maybe that was the surprise she spoke of. Do you have any suspects?"

"We don't have any suspects right now, but we're going to do a DNA analysis of the fetus. Hopefully, we can find the father from the DNA and ask him some questions."

Martina said, "You don't remember the name or ever seeing somebody with Lori?"

"No, but one time I heard the girls arguing. Este didn't like him. Whoever this guy was. But for some reason, they kept it a secret. From what I gathered, Este didn't think this boy was treating Lori right."

I nodded. "Is there anything else you can think of that could help us?"

"No, it was like one day they were here and then they were gone."

"Is there anybody else we need to notify?"

"I have some relatives. I'll let them know. When will we be able to have a funeral for the girls?"

Martina patted Mrs. Cruz on the shoulder and sat back down on the couch next to me. "We can't release the bodies yet because the medical examiner still needs to confirm who is who. We'll need dental records for that, but I'll let you know as soon as we can."

"Thank you for finding them." She shook her head again and teardrops fell one by one. I glanced at Martina, who nodded as if it was time for us to go. I stood up, Martina followed.

"Mrs. Cruz, is there anything else we can do for you?"

She looked up and patted her cheeks once again. "No, thank

you both. But you will keep in touch and let me know when I can have a service?"

"Of course. I'll let you know as soon as you're able to do that."

"May God bless the two of you."

With that, we exited the Cruz home. It should not have taken twenty years for someone to look for them or to find them or to find who hurt them. And we wouldn't stop until we did just that.

14

MARTINA

During the drive, it hit me. The photo album. Distracted by delivering the terrible news to Mrs. Cruz, it had slipped my mind that we'd planned to pick it up during the visit. If we hadn't just notified her that her nieces were murdered, I'd have Hirsch turn around and go back. But Mrs. Cruz needed time to process. At this point, the extra photos wouldn't be as important. In a few days, we'd go back to check on her and request it.

Hirsch said, "This is it. Bayou is clearly long gone."

We knew that, but the storefronts looked rather new. We stepped out and headed to the first establishment. The young woman in a green apron wasn't old enough to have been working twenty years ago. But that didn't mean I shouldn't ask if any of her coworkers might've been or if she knew how long the coffee shop had been in this location or to order myself a coffee while I was there. When in Rome?

"What can I get you today?" the cheery young woman asked.

"Hi, my name is Martina Monroe, and this is my partner, Detective Hirsch, from the CoCo County Sheriff's Department."

The young woman's smile vanished, as if I had just told her she was about to be arrested. Her eyes widened.

I said, "We'd like to ask you a few questions."

"Okay..."

"We're looking for anyone who may have worked around here twenty years ago or had frequented the Bayou Restaurant that used to be a few doors down. I'm guessing you weren't around here twenty years ago?"

She shook her head emphatically. "No. I'm only sixteen."

"Do you know how long this shop has been here? Or if anyone who works here also worked here twenty years ago?" I asked.

"I'll get the manager. He might." The young woman hurried away and returned with a man with dark hair, a white shirt, and also wearing a green apron. And not likely old enough to be of help.

"Hi, I'm the manager, Peter. Angela said that you had some questions about the restaurant?"

"Yes. I'm Martina and this is my partner Detective Hirsch, and we're investigating the murder of a young woman who used to work at the Bayou Restaurant twenty years ago. We're asking around the shops to see if anybody remembers any of the staff at Bayou or the young woman."

"Oh, well, I kind of remember the restaurant being here, but this shop didn't open until about fifteen years ago. The pizza place a few doors down used to be Bayou. The nail salon is pretty new, too. Actually, all the shops in this part are less than twenty years old. Don't quote me on that, but I'm pretty sure."

"Did you ever dine at Bayou?"

"No, I was just a kid. Middle school."

He looked like he was in his early thirties. "Well, you've been really helpful." Hirsch pulled out a business card and handed it to the man. "If you can think of anything that could help, call us."

"Of course. What was the woman's name?" the manager asked.

"Her name was Lori, and she was from Louisiana."

"Doesn't ring any bells. I'm sorry we couldn't be more help. Is there anything else I can get you while you're here? Maybe a little afternoon pick me up on the house?"

"Sure. I'll have a small black coffee."

The man nodded with a smile. "That's easy enough. And you, sir?"

"I'd love a caramel macchiato. If it's not too much trouble."

"No trouble."

Angela said, "I'll get it."

We thanked them both and stepped back. "Not terribly helpful, but at least we scored a free coffee."

Hirsch smirked. "One perk of being in law enforcement."

"Besides the fame and prestige and all the riches."

He chuckled. "If only."

We retrieved our coffees and headed out to question the other shops, but we came up empty-handed and confirmed what the manager at the coffee shop had stated — none of them had been around twenty years earlier. Between the lack of witnesses and the owners of Bayou, James and Vickie Barlowe, yet to return our calls, we weren't getting very far. "Do you think maybe the owners of Bayou are on vacation? It would make sense, right?"

"Yeah, unless they aren't getting back to us for a reason."

What motive would they have not to talk to us? Could they have something to do with Lori and Este's murders? Maybe the owner was the father of Lori's baby? It would certainly be a motive. We knew it was a husband and wife who had been running the restaurant. It would explain why Lori's boyfriend would have been kept secret. "What are you thinking?" Hirsch asked.

"Well, if they're not on vacation, perhaps they had something to do with Lori's death. Perhaps an affair with the boss? It would be a solid motive. Mr. Barlowe gets the girl pregnant and kills her so the wife doesn't find out?"

"Maybe. We'll have Vincent do a deeper dive on the owners."

It was as if we had one mind. "Agreed. There's another few hours of daylight if you want to head over to the park and ask around about Whitlock." According to the map, the park where Whitlock was killed was only two miles away.

"Let's do it. I need to make sure I have updates for Sarge and Lafontaine."

We pulled up to the park with lush green grass, giant redwood trees, a jungle gym, swings, picnic tables, and benches. It was a lovely park and no longer resembled a bloody crime scene. We hopped out of the car, and having already finished my coffee, I tossed the paper cup in the trash. "Let's split up."

"I'll go door-to-door to the surrounding houses. You take the folks in the park. Maybe we'll get lucky and find a nanny or two who has been working around here for a while."

I nodded and headed toward the first woman wearing joggers and a T-shirt with her hair in a messy bun. She was sitting on a bench, staring out at the playground. Undoubtedly at one of the children. "Hi, my name is Martina Monroe, and I'm with the CoCo County Sheriff's Department. May I ask you a few questions?"

"Sure, no problem. But I need to keep an eye on George. I'm the nanny."

Perfect. It was as if Hirsch knew what he was doing. "Great. I'm investigating a crime that was committed here in this park ten years ago. Were you working in the area ten years ago?"

"I was. George is from my second family. My first family's children are now grown up and one is in college."

"Did you only bring the children to the park during the day, or did you ever come at night?"

She shook her head. "The only ones who come at night are teenagers who come to drink and smoke pot. That kind of thing."

"Do you remember seeing or hearing about anything strange happening around ten years ago?"

She stared out at George but then furrowed her brow. "Wait. Ten years ago. That was when that man was stabbed and killed. Is that the crime you are investigating?"

"That's correct."

"They never caught the murderer?"

"No, they didn't. I'm trying to find somebody who remembers anything that seemed unusual or out of place around the time of the man's death."

"I don't remember anything, but I only visit the park during the day. You might have better luck coming here at night and seeing what elements show up. One of my kids, who's in college now, said that he would come to the park with his buddies and drink. That's how I know. The kids tell the nanny more than their parents," she said with a smile. The concern on my face must have shown. "Oh, not all kids. Do you have children?"

"I have a ten-year-old daughter. She used to have a nanny, but my mother lives with us now and takes care of her while I'm working."

Would Zoey confide in my mother instead of me? Would she drink at night at a park with boys?

The nanny said, "I'm sure your daughter is very good. Plus, you're an investigator. How much could she hide from you?"

How much indeed. I remembered being a teenager and not wanting to share any information with my mother or any authority figures. Would Zoey be the same? Gosh, I hoped not. Although she was clever, sometimes too clever for her own good. The school had labeled her gifted, which could be very dangerous. I only hoped Zoey used her smarts for good and not evil. She exhibited no signs that she was going toward the dark side. My girl was too pink and sparkly for that. Plus, she loved animals and people and art and glitter. "Is there anything else you can think of that might help our case?"

"No, like I said, maybe come back and see who is here late at night. Most of the other people here are parents, and only one other nanny." She pointed at a young blonde woman pushing a toddler in a swing. "But you can tell she's very young. I don't think she was here ten years ago unless she was a kid herself."

"Do you know the people who live in the surrounding houses? My partner is going door to door now to ask the neighbors if they saw anything."

"They didn't do that the first time?"

"They did, but sometimes when enough time has passed, people are more willing to talk to the police."

She nodded. "I understand. It's like that in my neighborhood, too."

"You don't live around here?"

She shook her head and laughed. "I live in Brentwood."

The amusement was no doubt the thought of a person on a nanny's salary affording this affluent neighborhood. "No kidding. I grew up on Stone Island, but I don't live there now."

"Good for you for getting out of that place."

My thoughts exactly.

I took down the woman's information and thanked her. She had some really good points like visiting at night when the crime was committed. But we were in the area and figured we'd stop by. You never know what you may find. We would have to return another night.

After interviewing the other visitors at the park, I walked away empty-handed, as the nanny had suggested I would. After I spotted Hirsch knocking on the door of the house just across the street, I ran up. "Any luck?"

"No. I think many people are at work. How about you?"

"Only one helpful nanny who suggested we ought to come back and question those who hang out at the park at night."

"And people will be home."

I nodded. "It's getting late anyhow. Let's head back, and we can plan a night visit later this week. I have a little girl to hug and hope she doesn't grow up to be a teenager who drinks and smokes pot in the park. Apparently, that's what the kids do."

"Crossing my fingers for you, but not holding my breath," he joked.

Was it true that all teenagers were terrible? Even my Zoey? She had been the light of my life since the first time I laid eyes on her. We were best buds, and she always wanted to know everything about my day and to tell me all about hers. She was growing up, and I worried how long I would have that part of her. She was getting more independent, was having her own ideas about things, and no longer idolized me like she once had. Her newest idol was Kim, Hirsch's wife. A kindergarten teacher who also loved pink sparkles. Glancing over at Hirsch, I said, "Thanks," sarcastically. He'd better be careful he didn't jinx himself.

15

HIRSCH

Weary from the day, I drifted toward Sarge's office without thinking. "Not heading back into the squad room?" Martina asked.

Clearly, I had too much on my mind and it showed. "No, I need to update Sarge. He agreed to keep the case quiet, but I told him I would give him daily updates." And after a call from Kiki five minutes earlier, we had a big one.

Martina nodded. "If I don't see you before I leave, have a good night."

"You too." Upon arrival at Sarge's office, I peeked inside. As usual, Sarge sat behind his desk, but he was on the phone. I retreated. He raised his hand and then just a finger, indicating he would be done in a minute and for me to not leave.

Sarge had been completely supportive of our under-wraps operation. I wondered if he knew more than he was letting on or was worried that we'd uncover another departmental cover-up. One of the first cases Martina and I worked together was just that. A retired sergeant had been covering for his son, a serial killer, making it seem as if a string of teenage girl disappearances were all runaways by assigning each missing person case to a different detective, so they couldn't connect them. We ended up taking down the whole rotten bunch. Those who were still alive anyhow. But it had left a stain on the department.

The Cold Case Squad was so new back then we didn't make enormous waves. Considering all the people who were associated with the cover-up were no longer with the CoCo County Sheriff's Department. But that didn't mean those folks who weren't there anymore weren't part of something bigger, like maybe generations of corruption within the Sheriff's Department or local PD. These days, we couldn't discount anything until we could, in fact, rule it out. It was one reason I was so cautious about the case, knowing that the responding officer was related to a prominent politician who was rumored to be running for the governor's seat.

Sarge hung up the phone and waved me in. I shut the door behind me. "How's it going?"

"Not bad. We confirmed the identity of the remains with DNA and dental records. We found Este and Lori."

"Not bad at all. Nice work. Any leads?"

I shook my head. "We're questioning businesses around Lori's former place of work, but the establishments are too new, and nobody was around back then."

He nodded. "Can you rule out any political connections yet?"

"Not yet."

"Well then, carry on, quietly."

I turned to leave, when he stopped me. "Actually, I'm glad you're here."

"Oh?"

Sarge knitted his eyebrows together and scratched the back of his bald head. "The sheriff told me he ran into you and that you're working on the Whitlock case."

"You didn't tell him we were working the case?"

"No."

Puzzled, I cocked my head. Sheriff Lafontaine knew a lot about that case, and I had assumed that Sarge had updated him. Who told him?

"What is it?" Sarge asked.

"When I spoke with the sheriff, he seemed to know a lot of details about the case. He brought it up. Not me."

He shook his head. "No, I didn't tell him about it. But he doesn't want you and Martina working on it."

"Why?"

He raised his hands as if he was defending the sheriff. Why would the sheriff care? I mean, it was his department, but what was wrong with working the Whitlock case?

"In his own way, it's a compliment. The sheriff thinks that you and Martina should work on a higher profile case, one that makes headlines. You know what I'm saying."

Was I buying this?

"So, the Whitlock case isn't newsworthy enough, and he wants us to work something that will get him some good press?"

"You're a quick one, Hirsch."

Shutting my eyes, I breathed out my mouth, inhaled deeply, and exhaled again. Martina had taught me her breathing techniques to calm her down when she was frustrated or angry. It worked — a little. "What would Sheriff Lafontaine like us to work on?"

"I'm so glad you asked. You can keep the Gomez sisters' case, quietly, but give the Whitlock case back to Jayda and Ross. He said not to work on it, but if they already have their fingers on it, they might as well run with it. But as for the new case, he said he'd pick it by next week. So, stay tuned."

Shaking my head at the ridiculousness, I said, "Great."

"It's not the first time, and it likely won't be the last time he does this. But like I said, take it as a compliment. He knows you and Martina solve the toughest cases, so he will probably pick a big one that will earn you plenty of headlines. You know the drill."

That I did, and I could only imagine what Martina's response would be. "Okay then." I didn't move out of the chair despite having ended the conversation. I was really tired of all the politics and having to continue to play the sheriff's games.

After I mustered my mental strength, I lifted myself off the chair. "Let me know when the sheriff has picked our new case. I'll let my partner know. She will be delighted."

That got a snort out of Sarge. "I can only imagine."

"Goodnight, Sarge."

"You too."

I waved and headed back to the Cold Case Squad Room. Martina was still there. Not to my surprise, she was talking in the corner with Vincent. I joined them, assuming they were talking about the case. "Hey. What's up?"

"Vincent was just telling me we need to do a deep dive on the owners of the Bayou."

"Yeah, put a rush on that." When I said it, I felt immediately foolish. Vincent rushed everything. I was tired and needed to get out of there so I could hug my wife. It had been a long day.

"You got it, boss."

"What's up, Hirsch?" Martina asked, no doubt using that intuition of hers. I explained to the two of them what Sarge had said about the Whitlock case and the selection of the replacement case.

Martina gave me a look that could kill a giant. I said, "I know. Sarge says we should take it as a compliment. He says it shows that he knows we can solve the tough cases. The cases that he can splash all over the news, making him and the department look good."

"I've heard that line before."

"When will you get the details of the sheriff's selection?" Vincent asked.

"He said no later than Monday."

"I guess I'll be handing off all of our notes back to Jayda and Ross?"

"They can handle it." And they could.

Martina shook her head. "That's not the point."

I knew it wasn't, and I knew Martina was frustrated with the sheriff's department. Having dealt with the bureaucracy my entire twenty-year career, I was bothered by it but also knew red tape and politics were Martina's mortal enemy. I thanked her recent suspension for that. It concerned me she would quit the Cold Case Squad and remain at her firm, where they respected her and knew how valuable she was. She came back, but I worried she would only take so much of the political power plays and return to Drakos, where she could continue to solve tough cases without worrying about being chastised by the brass. She was top-notch, and we worked really well together. We were both good independently, but together it was synergistic, our combined effect greater than the sum of our separate efforts. And I didn't want to lose that.

16

LORI

With my cheek resting on his chest, I squeezed him tighter. I had never felt closer to anyone except, of course, my twin sister but not a man or any other person outside of my family. Freddie and I were connected. Basking in the afterglow, I was full of joy that I could give my virginity to my first love. My only love.

I climbed up and planted a kiss on Freddie's lips. He stirred but didn't wake. He was out like a light. It was so cute. He had fallen asleep immediately after, but for me, it was as if something awakened inside of me. And I needed to do something with this new energy, but I wasn't sure what. I didn't want to disconnect from Freddie, but I wouldn't mind taking some time to take in the surroundings and maybe prepare a snack or dinner for Freddie once he woke up.

I untangled myself and slipped out of the bed. On my tiptoes, I walked over to my overnight bag and slipped on the black satin nightgown I had bought especially for the occasion. It was our two-month anniversary, and Freddie insisted on taking me on a weekend getaway to his parents' cabin in Arnold. It was a part of California that I hadn't explored yet. They called it the gold country. I thought it got the nickname because of the golden hue on the hills, but Freddie explained it was because they used to mine for gold during the gold rush of the 1840s.

Wearing nothing but my sexy lingerie, I strolled into the kitchen and made my way to the refrigerator. It was full of fruit, cheese, and sandwich fixings. There was a small market nearby, and we had decided we would pick up more provisions for dinner or go out to one of the few restaurants in town. It was as if yesterday, or even that morning, I was a child and now I was a woman with a boyfriend who had sex and stayed in a cabin by ourselves.

If anyone would have told me six months ago that I would be standing in that spot, I wouldn't have believed it. I had been so focused on my studies and what my future looked like, but it didn't include a man, at least not soon.

Feeling loose, I grabbed the open bottle of Chardonnay and refilled my glass that sat on the counter. I took a sip and studied the kitchen. It was rustic with its dark cabinets and tile counter-tops. Would Freddie and I have our own kitchen like this one day? I turned to the living room that had the most comfy sofa and gorgeous floor-to-ceiling windows.

Wine in hand, I curled up on the sofa, covered myself with the plaid blanket, and admired the view. The biggest trees I'd ever seen surrounded the cabin. Tall and green, it was like a fairyland. If only Este could see me there. All of her fears about Freddie would fly out the window when she saw how deliri-ously happy I was.

Our love bubble was cozy and warm, but I also really wanted to meet his friends and family. We had discussed the idea a few times, but he insisted it wasn't a good time for his family. I hadn't pushed as hard as I wanted to. It just made little sense to me, and he never made it any clearer. How busy could they possibly be? Everyone had to eat. I could slip in for a quick dinner. Didn't he want them to meet me? Or was it they didn't want to meet me? Maybe he hadn't explained how close the two of us had become.

Este thought it was a red flag. But I wasn't so sure about that. I thought maybe it was that Freddie was cautious about who he brought home. But he'd told me he had never been so in love before. Maybe he was scared we wouldn't work out in the end? Did he think I would break his heart? That was so sweet. But I couldn't discount Este's feelings.

What if it was reversed? What if it was Este dating a new guy I barely knew? How would I feel if he didn't have dinner at the house or wouldn't introduce Este to his family? I would be worried.

Feet pattered on the hardwood floors. I turned to see Freddie with tussled hair and wearing nothing but a pair of black boxers. He gave me that winning smile. "There you are."

"I'm just enjoying the view. It's so beautiful here."

He plopped on the couch and cuddled under the blanket with me. "I'll say." He kissed me passionately. After, he said, "I think I could stay like this forever."

"Me too."

We were wrapped around each other when the telephone on the wall rang. Freddie shut his eyes and huffed, as if annoyed. He untangled himself, hopped off the couch, and ran over to the kitchen. After Freddie picked up the receiver, he turned his back to me so I couldn't read his body language. Who knew we were here and who would call?

Less than a minute later, I jumped at the sound of Freddie slamming down the phone back into its base. He returned to the couch red-faced.

"Who was that?"

"Nobody," he snapped.

Concerned, I said, "It didn't seem like nobody."

"I don't want to talk about it."

"You know you can tell me anything."

He ignored my attempts at comforting him. He picked up my glass of wine and drained it. I placed my hand on his shoulder, and he turned away. Whoever had called had upset him quite a bit. I wished he would share with me. This was the first time I'd seen him like this, and I didn't know how to react properly. Should I give him his space or try to get him to talk? When he stood up and left the room, I supposed I had my answer. He needed space. The sound of the shower echoed in the cabin. I hoped a nice hot shower would improve his mood.

An hour later, I was in the kitchen fixing a snack when Freddie reemerged.

"I'm making a sandwich. Would you like one?"

His eyes were puffy, like he'd been crying. The blue irises glowed against pink sclera. This new side of Freddie was throwing me for a loop. Who was that on the phone? And what horrible thing had they said to him?

"Sure."

Turkey and cheese sandwiches complete, I set them on dishes and brought them to the dining table where he sat quietly. "Here you go." I placed his in front of him.

He mumbled what sounded like thanks.

Seated across from him, I picked up my sandwich and took a bite. Upon the last morsel, I wiped my fingertips on a paper napkin. He hadn't even looked at me once since returning from the shower. "Is everything okay?"

"Yeah. It's fine."

"Do you want to talk about it?"

"It's not important. Just some family stuff."

"Well, you can tell me. I mean, if one day we were married, they'd be my family too, right?" I said with a hint of joking.

He stared at me. "Married? We're not getting married."

My chest tightened. We hadn't exactly talked about

marriage, but we were in love, and we had never discussed not being together. Did he not love me like I loved him? Too stunned to speak, I sat still and tried not to cry. Had I been so stupid? Was Este right? He was only after one thing and once he got it, he would be gone?

Despite my efforts, the tears fell. Embarrassed, I hid my face in my hands as I sobbed. The sound of his chair scraping on the floor and his footsteps followed by the front door slamming shut was like a torpedo heading straight to my heart.

17

MARTINA

Ross and Jayda looked disappointed that Hirsch and I would no longer help with the Whitlock case, even though they tried to act like it wasn't a big deal. Or I was reading the situation wrong. Maybe the disappointment was that the sheriff thought we were too skilled to waste our time on the case, but Ross and Jayda weren't. I didn't think that was true at all. And I didn't for one minute believe the sheriff was paying us a compliment. Considering he no longer bothered to make eye contact with me. This did not add up.

Maybe he was setting us up to fail. Maybe the case he gave us would be impossible to solve and he would use that against us, or me, specifically. We were darn excellent investigators, but I would tell anyone who asked, there was some luck involved in solving cold cases. Eventually, our luck would run out and we would not close out a case. Maybe the sheriff knew that. Or he was betting on it. If he could argue that I didn't provide value, then it would be adios Martina.

It was the most likely reason he was overly involved in our cases. Or even in which cases we worked. Why would he care if we worked the Whitlock case? We could take on whatever case he gave us, plus investigate the Whitlock murder. From what Hirsch and Sarge explained, in the past, the sheriff hadn't involved himself with individual cases. Nothing about this turn of events sat right with me.

"But we can still keep investigating the case, right?" Jayda asked.

"The sheriff didn't say to stop, just that Hirsch and I couldn't work on it."

Jayda adjusted the necklace around her neck, straightening it out to show the diamond solitaire. "He didn't give any reason?"

"Sarge said it's not newsworthy enough." Jayda wrinkled her nose. "You know, it kinda makes me want to solve it even more and then hold a press conference."

"We'll solve it," Ross declared.

"If it's the last thing we do," Jayda added with a smile.

"I have no doubt. And I look forward to seeing the look on Lafontaine's face when you do."

Hirsch walked up to us. "How's it going?"

"Good. We're just talking about the Whitlock case."

"Hirsch, we will solve it."

"Of course you will."

"I was downloading to them all we've learned and the research we requested."

Jayda said, "You did quite a bit over the last few days."

"We did what we could." Part of me felt bad for giving the case back and had wanted to complete as much as I could for Ross and Jayda's sake. The other part wanted to solve it before handing it back or at least getting them close to the finish line so we could rub it in the sheriff's face. In the nicest way, of course.

"It's appreciated."

Turning to Hirsch, I said, "Has the sheriff picked our case yet?" It was so stupid that we were 'waiting' on a case to work. It was a complete undermine of Sarge and Hirsch's authority.

Hirsch shook his head. "No word from the sheriff yet. Sarge says we may not hear until Monday."

Ross shifted in his seat. "Boy, the sheriff sure loves the two of you. Giving you handpicked cases, I bet he misses seeing your face on the six o'clock news."

I said, "That may be, but my latest contract has a clause regarding the press. I no longer do appearances. We don't need that kind of recognition. God forbid some nut job shows up at my house or approaches Zoey."

"Oh, I get it. I don't blame you," Ross said.

The door creaked open, and I leaned over to see who it was. If it was one of the squad members, they would've just barged in like it was their home. After all, it was.

Kiki poked her head in, waved, and then shut the door. She was getting the hang of this whole covert operation business. I flicked Hirsch's arm. "Let's take a walk."

With a puzzled look on his face, he said, "I could always use more exercise, I suppose."

He obviously hadn't seen Kiki. I said, "We'll catch up with you two later."

The door on the other side of the room opened, and Vincent swaggered in. "Have I got something for you two?" He looked over at Jayda and Ross and back at us.

Hirsch said, "We're just about to take a walk. Why don't you come with us?"

I gave him a nod and a knowing look. "I like this whole walking and talking thing. They say that sitting is the new smoking."

Ross laughed. "Noted."

Vincent turned to head toward the door he'd come in. I said, "We're going the other way."

Vincent nodded slowly. "Yeah, the views from this way are more scenic."

Not very subtle. Based on the side-eye, I'd say Ross and Jayda noticed.

When we could, we would tell them everything, but it wasn't time yet. After a sharp inhale, I led the charge.

We exited from the right and found Kiki in the hall, staring at her cell phone. "Hey."

She glanced up. "Hey. Let's go out back and get some air."

She must have something good if she didn't want to tell us inside the building.

Outside, Kiki said, "Thanks for meeting me out here. I didn't want to risk going past the sheriff's office."

Smart. "What's up?"

"We finished analyzing the baby's DNA."

My heart raced. Had she identified the father? The killer?

"There is no match in CODIS."

Deflated, I said, "So, the father either didn't commit any violent crimes after killing Lori and Este or didn't kill them at all?"

"Or they haven't caught him yet," Vincent added.

Hirsch said, "It's not likely a person commits a double murder and then walks the straight and narrow."

"But it happens."

Vincent nodded. "True, plus, Dr. Scribner said the killer was likely inexperienced, and this was probably his first kill, between the botched strangulation and the messiness of the knife wounds. So, maybe he regretted it and never did it again. Maybe he killed Lori for whatever reason and regretted it but then had to kill Este because she was a witness. Who knows, maybe he turned his whole life around and is an upstanding citizen now. Atoning for his sins and whatnot."

"Vincent, our resident optimist," I joked.

Hirsch added, "Or he's simply a first-time offender who isn't in the system. Or the father is a dead end. We need to find other suspects."

Kiki said, "I wouldn't be too discouraged. We still haven't finished testing the evidence collected from Este. We might get lucky. Whoever killed them may have left their DNA behind on her clothing or under her fingernails. The original examiner took fingernail clippings, but because of the age of the remains, there may not be much left, but you saw there are plenty of bloodstains on her clothing. It could give us something. I need to take multiple samples. It will take some time."

Vincent said, "Hmm. So Paul Xavier is not the father of the baby. Then who?"

"What do you mean, he's not the father? He's a politician and likely hasn't committed any crimes or hasn't been caught. That, of course, doesn't mean he didn't father the baby. Why do you think he isn't the father?" Kiki asked.

"Because when I was doing a background on Xavier and his family, I found an article where he was swabbing for DNA. It was a stunt for the press. There was a missing person, later found dead, from his neighborhood, and he was trying to encourage everybody to submit DNA samples to be eliminated as suspects. The article had an explanation of how DNA identification worked and had a whole bit on CODIS and said that everyone who was swabbed would have their DNA in CODIS, including Xavier."

Kiki said, "Well, if that's true and they really put his DNA into CODIS, you're right, Xavier is not the father of the baby."

"Maybe we don't need to keep this quiet anymore."

Hirsch said, "If there is no connection to Xavier, maybe not. It would make things easier."

Vincent said, "Not so fast."

"Why? What else do you have?" I asked.

With a gleam in his eyes, Vincent said, "Something very interesting."

18

HIRSCH

Adrenaline shot through me. What else had Vincent found? He had dark circles under his eyes, and he looked like he hadn't slept in days. I was going to have to talk with him because it looked to me like he was working around the clock. He wasn't supposed to be. We needed him fresh and alert. At 100% Vincent in all of his glory. Not that he had made any mistakes, but I needed to ensure our best researcher didn't burn out.

Martina said, "What did you find?"

"Well, as you know, we identified four Jane Does who could be a potential match to Este and Lori. We knew two of them wouldn't be the sisters. But between us, I knew exactly which Jane Does were Este and Lori based on height, weight, where they were found, and their other characteristics. Because it was so simple, it got me thinking."

"About what?" I asked, still trying to figure out his big reveal.

"Well, when you find a Jane Doe with no identification, you try to identify them, right?"

"Right."

"What do you do next?"

Where was he going with this? "You check the missing persons database to see if there's anybody who matches the description of the Jane Doe."

Vincent nodded with a grin. "Exactly."

"And?" Martina asked, emphatically. Her impatience was on full display.

"So, I searched the missing persons database for Jane Does Two and Four, the ones we know aren't the Gomez sisters. I didn't get any hits — they are still unidentified. We'll need to identify them. Anyway, then I got curious and searched for Este and Lori's profiles on the database. You know, to see how the departments who found their remains could have missed the match."

I still didn't understand where he was going with this. "And?"

"I would guess that they missed the match for a few reasons. One, their disappearance wasn't splattered all over the news. Nobody knew they were missing, right?"

I really hoped he was getting to the point, and soon. "Right."

"But I think the real reason they missed the match was because Este and Lori Gomez are not listed on the missing persons database."

I stepped back and crossed my arms across my chest. "You mean they're not listed on the missing persons database now or they never were? It's protocol that every single missing person gets input into the database. It was mostly paper back then, but a few years ago, there was a huge initiative to transfer all paper records into the electronic system."

"From what I could see, they did not enter them. Ever. Now, we have to ask ourselves why weren't they on the missing persons database?"

It was a great question, and I didn't like the possible

answers. There was no acceptable reason for two missing persons to not be given a chance to be found.

Martina looked at me. "This is either really sloppy police work or somebody intentionally covered up their disappearance and their murders."

Vincent said, "Exactly."

But who would've covered up their murders? The father of the baby we had yet to identify? I didn't like this one bit. And I thanked the universe that Vincent had found it. If we dropped our cover and broadcast the homicide investigation on the news and it had been covered by someone with political connections, the investigation could be squashed. Like the sheriff had halted our involvement in the Whitlock murder. "Have you finished the deep dive on the Bayou Restaurant owners?" Maybe the case would lead us back to Mr. and Mrs. Barlowe. Had they fled the state after the Gomez murders? Did they have connections to law enforcement that would have helped cover up their crimes?

"I found some preliminary things that seem strange, so I have my guys going a little deeper. I found some business dealings — real estate that seems fishy but not obviously connected to this case. But what we found so far is that the Barlowes only owned and operated Bayou Restaurant for five years before they shut down. After that, they had a string of other businesses before retiring to Florida. My team is investigating those businesses and their whereabouts. It's weird we haven't heard from them yet. It's been a couple of weeks."

"Any criminal history on either of them?" Martina asked.

"No."

"Any connection to law enforcement or politics?" Martina asked.

"I didn't find any obvious connections."

"If this really was some kind of intentional cover-up, then by whom?" I asked.

"Well, Lori was pregnant. Maybe the father didn't want her to be. Maybe she wanted the baby, and he figured if she wouldn't get rid of it, he'd get rid of her and the baby. The sister was collateral damage."

"You're probably right. If not that, it was a stranger abduction and killing. I can't think of any other motive." Hopefully, we weren't looking at another serial killer tied to the CoCo County Sheriff's Department. That was the last thing we needed.

My gut stirred that we were going down the right route, but considering there was only one route, it made me nervous that we might miss something. "How long will it take for the rest of the forensics testing to be complete?"

Kiki looked like she was mentally creating a schedule.

As she contemplated, I wondered how Sarge would respond to learning the two missing sisters weren't input into the missing persons database by one member of the department. Would it be another black mark on the department's reputation?

Mistakes like that didn't happen very often. And if my instincts were correct, this was intentional, but I didn't want to share that yet. Because if I was right, it meant that somebody connected to the original investigation was responsible for the murder of the sisters. Somebody leading back to the reporting officer, David Xavier.

We had put off interviewing the now retired officer so that he wouldn't be tipped off we were working on the case. Was he the killer or covering for the killer?

Kiki said, "Give me a week. I'll have one of my analysts help, but I'll disguise the case numbers. We'll work as fast as we can."

Vincent smiled, as if he had just saved the day. Which he

kinda did. "One more week to find out if we can identify our killer."

Kiki nodded. "I'll be able to let you know if anybody else was at the murder scene."

"Thanks, Kiki. Thank you, Vincent. I don't know what we would do without the two of you and, of course, Dr. Scribner."

Martina cleared her throat.

"And Martina too."

She smiled. "All right, so, Kiki, we'll talk to you next week."

"Vincent, you'll work on the Barlowes' background."

"I'm on it, boss."

In some ways, it felt like we were making progress, but in other ways, it felt like we kept hitting dead ends. Nobody from their college campus remembered seeing the girls with a boy or having a boyfriend. But one of them had been getting close to someone, considering the pregnancy. It bothered me we had a lot of assumptions but not a lot of facts. The facts were we had two murdered sisters, but we didn't know by whom or why.

19

MARTINA

Frustrated, I hung up the phone and walked over to the whiteboard. The Barlowes, the owners of Bayou Restaurant, had nothing in their past that could implicate them, such as a criminal record. Maybe they had nothing to do with Lori and Este's murders. But after interviewing professors and their aunt, the only other people active in their lives were the unnamed boyfriend and the Barlowes. That dwindled our pool of suspects down to a stranger, the boyfriend, and the Barlowes.

Vincent said, "You know, just because they don't have a criminal record or any obvious reasons to kill them, it doesn't mean they're innocent."

It was true. The absence of a criminal record didn't mean one wasn't a criminal. Vincent had also learned from the Barlowes' next-door neighbors, the couple were 'lovely' and were on a three-week vacation in Europe, not expected to be back for another few days. These facts made them appear a lot less suspicious. Not cleared, but less likely to be hiding something. But my gut, and the discovery that the Barlowes were actually on vacation, said to me they had nothing to do with

Lori's and Este's murders. All signs pointed to the secret boyfriend.

A secret boyfriend whose DNA wasn't in CODIS, therefore remaining a secret. We had blood to be analyzed by our friends in the lab from the killing of Este, but if our theory was correct and the boyfriend killed both sisters, we still wouldn't know his identity. That put us at square one of the homicide investigation. When the Barlowes returned from Europe, we would interview them, but if they didn't give us anything useful, we'd be stuck. Out of people to interview and no usable DNA.

If this were any other case that didn't have potential political ties, we would blast the girls' pictures on the news, asking for the public to come forward if they knew the Gomez sisters or if they had any information on their murders. If we could do that, maybe we'd get some classmates who remembered Lori with a boy around school. The twins were likely to be remembered by a few, since they were twins and took all the same classes. Surely, they were memorable. Who knows, maybe the baby's father would come forward if he were innocent, and we could trace their last steps. Or we could find their car. Anything that would bring us closer to finding the truth.

Hirsch walked in with a furrowed brow and matching frown. He had a white binder in his hands. He looked just about as grumpy as I had ever seen him. "Do you need to grab a coffee?"

"No, I don't think that will help."

"What's up?"

"I just finished a meeting with Sarge and the sheriff."

The spine of the binder read Gerald Ackerman Binder, One of Four. Of course. "Is that our new case, handpicked by the sheriff himself?"

Hirsch sighed. "Yep. What do you two have there?"

Vincent said, "Basically nothing. The Barlowes are totally

clean, and I talked to their neighbors. Apparently, the Barlowes are friendly, normal, nice, and on vacation in Europe until the end of the week."

"So, not likely our suspects, but they could be. We'll keep looking until we find something."

I don't know if I ever considered Hirsch to be the optimist of the two of us, but it looked that way. Enough about the sad state of the Gomez case. I had to be patient. "All right, let's hear it."

He set the binder down on the table and flipped it open. "Gerald Ackerman, age ten years old, went missing while riding his bike to school. The school was four blocks from his house. The bike and body were never found."

Vincent nodded. "I remember the case. It was all over the news. It's not a very old case."

If I recalled correctly, it was less than five years ago, and there was a state-wide search and interview effort that went on for nearly a year before they gave up. What else could we do? Nothing. And that was exactly what the sheriff was hoping for. Despite what some people thought, I didn't always like to be right.

Hirsch said, "He went missing five years ago."

My memory wasn't so bad after all. "I remember it. With four binders and national press coverage, it was investigated pretty thoroughly, with little-to no evidence to process."

Hirsch let out a heavy sigh. "You're right. They canvassed neighborhoods. They talked to every neighbor, friend, relative, acquaintance, or guy standing on the street. Flyers were posted on every corner, and they held candlelight vigils."

The exact opposite of what they did to find Lori and Este.

How could Sarge think this was a compliment? Was he following orders and was told to tell us this was a positive thing? If there was one thing Hirsch and I were not, it was a couple of egomaniacs. Telling us we were the best didn't blind us to what was really going on. That was what made us a great investigative team. Not that we could do it without our support staff, like Vincent, Kiki's team, and Dr. Scribner. Was Sarge on the sheriff's side? Did we need to keep details from him? Hirsch would never have agreed to that. Perhaps it was just one more thing I had to get used to, the inability to trust my superiors. The sheriff didn't need to work so hard. At this rate, I wouldn't renew my contract if the sheriff begged me to stay. I was no egomaniac, but I knew my worth. I didn't have to be at the sheriff's department to do good and bring answers to families.

Vincent said, "What's wrong, Martina? You look unhappy."

"Well, this doesn't make me very happy. I have a bad feeling that the Ackerman case will be a wild goose chase. And the sheriff knows it. And we have to work it instead of focusing on finding Lori and Este's killer." Saying the words aloud didn't make me feel any better. It just got me more worked up.

Hirsch eyed me. "What happened to that can-do attitude, Martina? We haven't even looked at the case files yet."

Trying to calm myself, I took a beat before saying, "It's been a long day. And I'm frustrated we haven't gotten closer to identifying Este and Lori's killer."

Hirsch said, "I understand. But with the Ackerman case, I don't think we should make any assumptions. We should go through all the binders. Maybe there's something that was missed. Fresh eyes. If anyone can find Gerald Ackerman, it's this team. And I know you know that."

Hirsch was convincing. And he was right. I was rushing to judgment based on my distaste for the sheriff and his shenanigans. There was a missing little boy out there, and we had to do our best to find him and bring him back to his family.

What a Monday. "You're right. We'll treat this like any other case that is handed to us. I'll start reading."

"It's almost five o'clock."

"It's not five o'clock yet. I'll read until then." Like a child, I huffed, sat down in front of the binder, and flipped open the cover.

Since they reinstated me, the sheriff imposed a strict policy about the number of hours I worked. Eight hours a day. No more, no less. If you asked me, the policy was just another way the sheriff was trying to kneecap me. If I couldn't work a few extra hours when needed, it could mess with the progress of the investigation. He was likely trying to point out I wasn't necessary and that I could leave the extra work to another member of the team. Unimportant was the message. All I could do at that point was prove him wrong. If he had wanted to poke this mama bear, he succeeded. I would find Gerald Ackerman if it was the last thing I did.

20

LORI

After wiping my hands off on my apron, I answered the phone. "Bayou, this is Lori. How can I help you?"

"It's me."

My nerves rattled. Was he going to cancel on me again?

After the cabin, we had hardly seen each other. After he stormed out, he apologized and explained he had some family things going on and that was why he'd acted like he had. He said he couldn't handle the pressure from his family and me. As usual, he wouldn't explain what family pressure he had, even though I just wanted to understand. I wanted to be there for him. Instead, he suggested we take a break and "cool off" for a while. The break was my heart. The cool was the vibes he emitted. I'm not proud of it, but I begged him to give us a chance. I swore there were tears in his eyes. He didn't want to end things. So, why was he acting this way? I had been hopeful I had gotten through to him, but he canceled our last date, and the last time we saw each other, he was moody and cut the date short, claiming he didn't feel well. Este thought he was blowing me off and that I should take the hint and the lesson. As if it was that easy to forget his declarations of love or the softness of his lips. Was it all fake?

"Hey. I can't wait to see you tonight." And it was true. I just couldn't accept it was over. The look of love in his eyes couldn't be faked, could it? Maybe it was something else going on with him he wasn't telling me. Este said I was being pathetic for still hanging on. That started an enormous, blow-up argument. She apologized but said she really thought it was over with Freddie and I should try to move on. She didn't understand what it was like. To feel loved and connected with another person. It couldn't be over.

"About that. I have a family thing I can't get out of."

We had seen each other exactly four times in the last eight weeks and had a dozen phone conversations. If he wanted to break up, why didn't he just say so? I was running out of tears and self-respect. Glancing around the empty restaurant, I decided it was time to get some guts. "Are you breaking up with me?"

"I think we should take a break."

"Like a break up?"

"If you want to call it that, yes, a break up."

The sadness turned to fury. "So, all these months of telling me you loved me was a lie? What was I to you? A roll in the hay? Well played."

"It wasn't a lie. Don't make this harder than it needs to be. We can't be together. And that's final."

My chest tightened, and I couldn't breathe.

Este was right. She'd been right all along. He never really loved me, and it was all an act. How had I been so stupid? How could I have fallen for him? Yes, he told me I was beautiful and smart and that he couldn't stop thinking about me. That he loved me. I thought we were connected, but I was wrong. I was a sucker. How could I ever trust myself with another man? I couldn't. I was done.

"Are you still there?"

Was I? No, the old Lori was gone and replaced with a hollow figure. "I have to go." And I hung up before I burst into tears. I didn't want to give him the satisfaction. Remembering where I was, I dried my eyes and guzzled a glass of water. I wasn't okay at that moment, but I would be. I hoped.

I picked up the rag on the counter and headed over to the tables to clean the tops. Wiping in a circular motion, my head swam. I took a deep breath and used the table to keep myself upright. I stood there until I heard the jingle of the door opening. Mrs. Barlowe hurried over. "Are you okay?"

"I feel lightheaded."

"You look pale."

Before I could speak, I ran to the back of the restaurant, pushed open the bathroom door, and hurled into the toilet.

From the doorway, Mrs. Barlowe said, "Are you sure you're okay? Did you have something bad to eat?"

Sitting on the dirty bathroom floor reminded me that my next chore at the restaurant was to clean the bathrooms. It was the grossest place I could be. Had Freddie broken me mentally and physically? Heartbreak and stress were known to cause physical symptoms. "No, it just suddenly hit me."

"Could you be pregnant?"

"No, of course not..." But then I paused and stared at the grimy grout on the tile. Mentally checking my calendar in my head, my stomach flipped. I hadn't had my period since before Freddie and I went to the cabin. We used protection. At least he told me he had put a condom on. Had it broken? I started laughing and I couldn't stop.

Of course. My first boyfriend just broke my heart. And there I sat on a dirty floor with sick on my shirt — pregnant with his child. Well, if I had any doubts about God before, this about solidified it. He didn't exist and if he did, he was having a laugh at my expense.

"Uh. Are you sure you're okay?"

Suddenly realizing I wasn't alone in my pity party, I stopped laughing like a hysterical person and wiped the tears away. "I'm fine. Sorry, I just realized I had a burger earlier. Este told me it didn't smell right. That'll teach me to eat at the school cafeteria."

"And to listen to Este!" she stated playfully.

"Indeed."

Feeling gutted, I forced a grin. What was I going to do? I was eighteen. Pregnant. And the father didn't want to have anything to do with me. What was I going to do?

Mrs. Barlowe said, "I'll call your sister and have her come pick you up. You should go home and rest."

I turned to look at her. "I appreciate that."

What would Este say? How would I tell her? "Hey, sis. Freddie dumped me, and I think I'm pregnant. What do you want to get for dinner?" Ugh. The thought of food made my stomach flip again. Maybe I wasn't pregnant. Maybe this was a wake-up call. Or food poisoning. It was time to get my act together. I remained on the bathroom floor crying, as quietly as I could, for twenty minutes, when a knocking noise drew my attention. I wiped my face with my sleeve and looked up.

"Oh jeez, you look terrible."

"Thanks, Este."

"Mrs. Barlowe said it was the burger?"

Tear drops fell. "Yeah, it was probably the burger."

Este's face morphed from worry to dread. "Oh, Lori."

I bowed my head and sobbed. Este ran over and held me. She knew it wasn't the burger, and so did I.

21

MARTINA

Huddled in our new, secret conference room, my mind was laser focused on Lori and Este while Hirsch gave Vincent and me the update from his discussion with the Barlowes. Besides describing their sun-soaked vacation in Greece, Mrs. Barlowe confirmed that Lori definitely had a boyfriend. He never visited the restaurant, but he had phoned there several times when Lori was working. Lori usually answered the phone, but once Mrs. Barlowe had, and when she asked who was calling for Lori, all he'd said was that it was her boyfriend. A little put off by the statement, Mrs. Barlowe didn't push further but had asked Lori later the name of her boyfriend.

"Did she tell you his name?"

"No, but get this. Lori's response was that she just referred to him as her guy. When Mrs. Barlowe asked why, Lori said it was because he always referred to her as babe or his girl but never by her name. She thought it was cute, so she started doing the same to him."

That wasn't cute at all. It was a sign of an abuser. Abusers don't call their victims by their given name as a way of controlling or dehumanizing them. Letting the victims know they no longer had their own identity. It wasn't a good sign. "I don't like the sound of that."

Vincent nodded. "That's a red flag for domestic violence, right?"

Vincent was in his mid-twenties and smart, but he didn't strike me as worldly. His astute observation surprised me a little. "Do you know a lot about domestic violence?"

"Not a lot, but I have come across articles while doing research and then started looking for patterns of domestic violence within witness statements in homicide cases. There are a lot of warning signs like isolation, love-bombing, gas-lighting, and never calling the victim by their name. That last one really stuck with me. That and the fact domestic violence happens to all genders and all walks of life. Basically, anyone in a relationship can fall victim."

Good for him. It was good to know the signs. My guess was Lori hadn't. "What else did they say about Lori?"

"That she was smart, good with customers from the start, and was never late."

"That's basically how the girls' professors described them, too. No one has had a single bad word to say about either of them."

Hirsch eyed me. If I could read his thoughts, they were, "Yeah, yeah, you said you always thought it was the boyfriend."

I smirked. "They never saw him picking her up after work or dropping her off?"

Hirsch shook his head with a look of disgust on his face. "No. Either they would meet at a location, or he would pick her up around the corner from her house but never at her house. Mrs. Barlowe said she tried to warn Este and Lori that wasn't normal behavior and to be more cautious. Este had agreed, but Lori brushed it off like it was no big deal and said Mrs. Barlowe was old fashioned."

How awful. What else had this boyfriend done to her? Besides, of course, most likely murdering her and her sister. Hirsch continued, "That's not all. Mrs. Barlowe was not surprised that Lori was pregnant. She said she had gotten sick at work. She tried to say it was food poisoning, but Mrs. Barlowe knew the signs and the look of terror in Lori's eyes when she suggested it to her."

Thinking back to the red flags and issues surrounding intimate partner violence, I recalled two of the most dangerous times for a woman in an abusive relationship were when they fell pregnant or tried to leave.

I wasn't a profiler, but the motive for Lori's murder was becoming more clear. Not one to draw conclusions without solid evidence, still, I had heard enough. He didn't call her by her name, didn't meet her at the house, and she was pregnant when she died. She was likely a victim of domestic violence, or, in this case, intimate partner violence. You don't have to live with somebody to be a victim. Unfortunately, it's very common for teenagers. We needed to find the boyfriend. When we did, we'd find who'd killed Lori and her sister. "All that confirms our suspicions and maybe adds a few data points."

"She was likely a victim before she was a victim," Vincent added.

"That's what I suspect. We need to find the boyfriend. But how?" As long as we had abusers, the Cold Case Squad would have a job to do.

Hirsch said, "We wait for the rest of the forensics, and if we get nothing, we'll have to interview David Xavier and ask about the case. If nothing strange crawls out of the woodwork, we have the green light to go public. Put their faces on every news station. We'll need the photo from their last day."

"When we get to that stage, I'll call Mrs. Cruz and ask her if she's okay with me picking it up." Again. But this time she wouldn't be hearing that her nieces were dead for the first time. Fingers crossed there was no cover-up or political ties. We were running out of options to find the Gomez sisters' killer. "Okay. We wait for Kiki."

"Next case. Gerald Ackerman. Where should be start?" Hirsch asked.

"I finished reviewing the records."

"Already?"

"Yep." It had been my secret bedtime reading for the previous two nights.

"Anything stand out?"

Nodding, I said, "There was something I found a little strange and surprising, too. As I suspected, the case had been thoroughly investigated. The team knocked on every door and talked to every neighbor, school official, other students, teachers, but there was not a shred of evidence against any of them. But there's one thing they didn't do which, in a case like that, I would think they would have."

"Vincent, did you read the files?"

"I'm about halfway through."

"Anything strike you as strange?"

"Maybe...." Vincent smiled, as if he knew exactly what I was about to say. "Let's hear what you think first, Martina."

"Well, one thing that stood out to me was that they didn't bring in the FBI or a profiler. They interviewed absolutely everybody but didn't have a profile for the perpetrator. Why? Stupidity? If we had a profile, we could match it against the witness statements. Our perp most likely gave a statement."

Hirsch said, "I agree."

Vincent smirked.

"What is it?"

Vincent leaned back. "It's pretty standard to bring in the

FBI for help in such a high-profile kidnapping. Why didn't they? Could it be a cover-up?"

Hirsch shook his head. Was he tired of us suspecting a problem within the department? Hey, if the evidence fit. "I asked the same question when I read the files. Lafontaine was in his first term as sheriff. He was young, and some doubted his ability. I think they didn't ask the FBI for help because he wanted to solve it himself — to make himself look good. He didn't want to look incompetent."

And then it hit me, and it made me sick. "He was too proud to ask for help. He tried to do it himself, and by doing that, he let a kidnapper get away?"

Hirsch said, "I think that's the most likely case. He's cocky now. Imagine what it was like his first year in office wanting everyone to think he was a star. Considering they reported Gerald missing within hours of his abduction, Lafontaine probably could've brought that child home five years ago if he had reached out to the FBI."

"I vote we reach out to the FBI."

Vincent raised his hand. "I second it."

Hirsch shrugged. "Well then, I guess that's the official vote."

Vincent shimmied his hands as if he were doing a jazz performance. "Lucky for us, we have ties to the FBI. I know people in the San Francisco office who would be happy to help. And they owe me a favor."

"Make the call."

"Will do." With that, he slid out of the room, likely feeling quite proud of himself.

"You seem pretty determined to solve this case."

"Hirsch, we will solve this case."

He chuckled. "There's that optimism I love."

22

MARTINA

Vincent was doing something that resembled a dance. Is that how people danced? Or was he losing his mind? "Are you hearing music, like right now?" I asked.

He threw his head back and laughed. "No, but I am dancing because I got good news for you about the Ackerman case," he sang.

Hirsch said, "We're all ears."

"I just talked to my friend at the FBI. She said we need an official request for their help. But... because we're buddies. Yes, I, Vincent Teller, have friends in high places." He paused for, I don't know, applause, laughter, effect? "Jess, or to the unfamiliar, Agent Jessica Holley, thinks the profile won't take long. I gave her some initial details about the case. She said she will start working quietly, but they need that official request, Hirsch."

"No problem. I'll write it up today."

"How long will it take to get the profile?" I asked.

"Jess said the profile won't be complex, but she also wants a copy of the case file to look at the witness statements. You've seen the case file. It will take a while. She will do what she can but won't be able to come down to talk to us any earlier than next week."

"That's pretty fast," Hirsch remarked.

"Well, like I said. I have friends in high places," he said with a smirk.

"Then I guess we're lucky to have you." Thanks to Vincent, we could solve the Gerald Ackerman case in record time. Not that I was doubting it too much before, but these connections meant we could narrow down the suspects. I had no doubt that the suspect was already in that file, but if we had a profile and could show it matched, we would have enough for a warrant to search their home. The previous investigators never had enough probable cause to search anybody's house or car or anything. We would change that.

"May I get that in writing?" Vincent joked.

I smiled.

Hirsch said, "You're pretty happy about this."

"I am. Mark my words. We will find Gerald Ackerman."

Hirsch said, "Oh, they're marked."

And we all laughed. It was good to laugh. It had been a little tense around the office since Vincent and my suspension, but things were getting back to normal.

Kiki poked her head inside the Cold Case Squad Room, and we silenced. I said, "C'mon in. We're the only ones here right now."

She walked inside with a file folder in her hand. "Is it okay to speak in here? I have some very sensitive information."

Adrenaline rushed through my veins. She had something good. "It's okay. The other teams are out for the rest of the day."

"May I use this whiteboard to explain the analysis that we conducted?"

Hirsch walked over to a whiteboard not in use and handed her a marker. "You can use this one."

"Thank you."

We stood around her and watched as she drew a diagram of what I was assuming was Este's body and the clothing they found her in. Kiki had labeled each of the garments A, B, C, and D and then recorded A, B, C, and D and started outlining all the different analyses she did on each piece and how many samples she took and where they were taken from the articles of clothing. She had been thorough, and she had worked fast, all things considered.

Studying Kiki as she continued, I realized she was younger than I had first assessed. She was likely in her early thirties and must not have been out of graduate school for long. Her energy on the case showed she wanted to solve these crimes just as badly as we did. I think sometimes investigators lost track of that. We thought we were the only ones who cared, but in my experience, everyone, from the receptionist to the research team and everyone in between, cared. I had to remember that the next time we celebrated a Cold Case Squad win. We needed to include everyone who had contributed to solving the case, like Kiki and Dr. Scribner.

After a few minutes, Kiki stepped back and pointed at a drawing of a scarf that had been wrapped around Este's neck. "This is the scarf that was used to strangle Este, but the perpetrator..." She shut her eyes, paused, and then opened them again. "He used it to kill her, but he failed. It takes several minutes to kill somebody through manual strangulation. Newbies rarely know this. It takes six minutes. He likely gave up before that. As you can see on her shirt, there are cuts. He made those with a two-and-a-half-inch blade, likely a pocketknife. It wasn't very long, and the chest wounds weren't deep enough to kill, but he tried. After several — ten — attempts, that didn't work either. So, he went for the neck. He nicked her carotid artery, through the scarf, and that led her to bleed out.

As you can imagine with this type of trial-and-error method, he was likely frustrated and careless. He probably cut himself during the attack or was sweating during the struggle because of stress and exertion. For that reason, we tested multiple samples from her clothing in the event he left a blood droplet or sweat or other DNA. To do that, we had to take pieces from her clothing. We cut them up into small pieces and analyzed every single one of them."

Vincent said, "Whoa, that's amazing."

"Just another day on the job."

"Am I the only here who's not modest?"

I said, "Yes, Vincent, you are the only one."

That made us all smile, but I quickly grew serious. "I'm guessing there's something you want to tell us."

Kiki said, "Yes. First, we found that there was no evidence of sexual assault. I conferred with Dr. Scribner, and we think it was strictly a murder."

"Like they needed to get rid of her because she witnessed Lori's murder?" I asked.

Hirsch nodded. "Exactly."

That was something. We had figured that was the case. Kiki said, "That's not all. On the red scarf, we found two DNA profiles. One we confirmed was Este, the second contributor was male." She paused and looked around the squad room. We were the only ones in the room. "We got a hit in CODIS for the male DNA."

My heart was ready to jump out of my chest. "The second DNA profile is a match for Paul Xavier."

Vincent stated the obvious. "The mayor of San Ramon who is running for the governor's seat?"

As stunned as we all were, Kiki continued. "Yes. After I got the positive match for the blood found on the red scarf, I went back and looked at the baby's DNA profile to see if Xavier was the father, in case I missed something the first time I ran the DNA through CODIS. There was no mistake. Paul Xavier is not the father of Lori's baby."

"Then why would he kill Lori and Este?" I asked the room.

"Secret serial killer?" Vincent offered.

"Serial killer turned mayor? I can see the headlines now," Hirsch said.

I stood with my hand on my hip, contemplating what this meant. What motive would Paul Xavier have to kill eighteen-year-old sisters? He wasn't the father of the baby. I didn't buy that he was some serial killer who turned into a politician. Although stranger things had happened. That didn't make sense, but it proved, to me anyway, that the missing persons case had been covered up. Most likely, Xavier used his cousin to botch the investigation and to not put their names in the missing persons database. Despicable.

I would get a lot of satisfaction from watching Hirsch cuff Xavier. Vincent said, "He's not the father of Lori's baby, and we don't think he was a blood-thirsty serial killer turned politician... Although when you think about it, it's not that big of a leap. Am I right?" Vincent searched for the laugh.

I gave him a look like this is not the time for joking.

Vincent said, "Okay, fine. No jokes. Maybe he was helping a friend or relative?"

Like a flash of light, it was clear. I said, "He was friends with the boyfriend." The boyfriend had to be involved. I could feel it in my bones.

"Have you ever had a friend willing to help you kill two people? What kind of friend is that?"

Hirsch stared off as if contemplating suspects. "They'd have to be thick as thieves."

23

HIRSCH

In a state of semi-shock, I was having a difficult time with the fact Paul Xavier had murdered Lori and Este. Why? And who knew about it? His cousin David Xavier — the responding officer and person who was responsible for putting the Gomez sisters' photos and profiles into the missing persons database — was he the boyfriend?

As painful as the covert nature of our investigation was, I was thankful we had kept it quiet. Would Lafontaine help cover up Xavier's crimes? Was Lafontaine connected to the crimes? Could Lafontaine be the boyfriend? He kept photos of his wife and two young children on his desk. In each family photo, Lafontaine looked like a proud father. Shiny and smiling. It didn't fit that Lafontaine would have murdered his pregnant girlfriend. I wasn't the sheriff's biggest fan, but he didn't strike me as a cold-blooded killer. That didn't rule him out as a person of interest, considering he lived in the area at the time of the Gomez sisters' deaths and was friends with their killer. Or at least, Este's killer. Lafontaine may not be a killer, but I'd bet a dozen donuts he'd do just about anything to make himself look good. Would he cover up his best friend's crime to not be implicated in the scandal?

"What are you thinking, Hirsch?" Martina asked.

"For starters, we need to be very careful. What are the odds that Lafontaine's best friend murdered someone, and he didn't know about it?"

Vincent scratched his chin. "You know, Lafontaine was one of the youngest sheriffs to be elected in recent history. Even if he didn't take part in the murders, if he found out Xavier killed the sisters, maybe Xavier and his family promised him a lightning rise to the top if he kept quiet. Xavier's family were strong supporters of his first campaign and second." Vincent shook his head. "Or maybe not. Based on my research, Lafontaine and Xavier were twenty-two at the time of the murders. Both were college students. They might not have planned their career paths that young. I know I didn't."

It was a good point, but it wasn't sitting right with me. "Xavier's family could've promised him whatever career he wanted after he graduated. Lafontaine's family was prominent in the community as well."

Martina said, "So, basically, the sheriff can't know about any of this until we execute search and arrest warrants."

"Exactly."

"Kiki, do you have any evidence left to test?" Martina asked.

"I do. There are some items, leaves and soil around Este's body, still to be tested. But when I saw the match for the blood droplets found on the scarf, I wanted to bring it to you right away."

I said, "Let's hope there's an additional DNA sample, or other evidence, that can help explain what happened that night. If our theory that he killed Lori near the water and then killed Este and drove her out to Calaveras County and buried her is correct, what happened to her car? Did Xavier drive her car to kill and dump Este? Or if our theory about the boyfriend being involved is correct, he would have had his own car, right? If that's right, we have two killers."

"Xavier has no logical motive. My bet is two killers," Martina added.

Two killers meant two motives. And twenty years where neither killer rolled on the other. Whoever killed alongside Xavier had kept quiet. He had to have been close to Xavier or Xavier had paid them off. Whatever the reason, my gut was telling me that even if we found Xavier's partner-in-crime, he wouldn't talk to us. We had DNA evidence against Xavier but no physical evidence connecting a second killer. Would Xavier's partner walk free? Or would Xavier implicate the other killer? Too many questions.

"We have enough for an arrest warrant, right?" Vincent said.

"The forensics will hold up, but we don't have a story. If we arrest Xavier, his accomplice or accomplices could scatter or start destroying any potential evidence or get together to make up a story. I'll bring this to Sarge, see what he thinks. We want a compelling story besides the hard evidence. We don't want Xavier out on bail."

There was already a lot going on in my personal and work life, and if Lafontaine was involved in covering up the murders, it could blow everything up. I hoped it didn't come to that. "Kiki, thank you for this. I'm going to go talk to Sarge and figure out our next move."

After the group wished me luck, I headed down to tell Sarge the news. Lafontaine enjoyed making headlines, but I didn't think he'd like this one. I stepped toward the door of Sarge's office and stopped dead in my tracks. Apparently, I wasn't very quiet since the man sitting across from Sarge turned around and looked at me. "Hey, Hirsch, how is it going?"

"It's going well, Sheriff. How are you?"

"Doing very well, thank you. Did you need Sarge for something?"

"It's not urgent. I can come back later."

"Feel free to say anything you need to in front of me. We don't have secrets here. You know that."

Sweat broke out on my temples. "Actually, it's not work related. Kim wanted to know if Sarge and Betty wanted to come over for dinner Saturday night."

"I'd have to check with Betty, but that sounds nice," Sarge said, with a puzzled look on his face.

"It's good that everyone gets along. Isn't it?" the sheriff asked with a sparkle in his eyes. The eyes of a person of interest in a double murder. If he weren't the sheriff, we would have him in an interview room asking him everything he knew about Lori and Este and his pal, Paul Xavier. But he was the sheriff and could bury this deep.

"Yes. Okay, then. I'll see you both later. Have a good night."

I turned around and headed back to the Cold Case Squad Room. Hopefully, Sarge could tell that I was not being truthful. Not that we wouldn't love to have them over for dinner, but it wasn't why I had stopped by.

"Back so soon?"

"He wasn't alone, so I invited him over for dinner Saturday night."

Vincent cocked his head.

"It was my cover. The sheriff insisted I talk to Sarge in front of him, since there are no secrets in the department. It was the only thing I could think of."

Martina cackled. "No secrets."

No kidding.

A few minutes later, Sarge walked into the squad room. "Dinner?"

I waved him in. "Not that we wouldn't love to have you over, but..."

"It's bad isn't it?" He winced.

We explained the situation. And Sarge's face and bald head lost a shade or two.

"I see why you didn't want to explain that in front of Lafontaine."

Without a word, Vincent rushed out of the room. We stood there in silence, likely all wondering what just happened. Vincent returned with an envelope. He set it on the table and spread out many photocopies of press releases and news reports that had photos of Xavier with Lafontaine. Vincent said, "Xavier's not the father of Lori's baby. But he killed Este. Why?"

"You don't think..." Sarge asked what we were all thinking.

"We don't know, but considering the close connection, either Xavier is a secret serial killer, or he was helping somebody else get rid of a problem. And considering his bestie is Lafontaine..."

It wasn't the only theory. I said, "Or Lafontaine could have known about the crime and promised to keep it quiet. Or he knew nothing about it but could try to bury the investigation so that the headlines didn't read 'Sheriff's BFF Arrested for Double Murder.'"

Sarge remained stoic. "I'm not convinced Lafontaine murdered anybody or covered up anything. He's not the devil, like some of you think. Let's not get ahead of the facts. I haven't heard a shred of evidence that Lafontaine's involved in this. Being friends with a killer doesn't make you a criminal. Let's not forget that. Also, I didn't hear any evidence that Xavier killed Lori. Just Este. You need to tie it all together. If he did kill Lori too, prove it. If not, figure out who did. That being said, there is enough reason to keep it quiet, especially from Lafontaine, until you put together a compelling story and get an arrest warrant for Xavier."

Sarge was right. We needed to make sure we got all the facts before jumping to conclusions. We had no physical evidence that Xavier killed Lori. "And how is your other case going? The one the sheriff does know about?"

"We've reached out to the FBI to get a profile on who may have taken Gerald Ackerman."

"They didn't do that five years ago?"

"No. They interviewed everybody within a fifty-mile radius, but they didn't get a profile. We're hoping a profile will match up with somebody already in those case files. We just have to figure out which one."

"Smart, and keep that quiet, too. Lafontaine doesn't like the FBI."

Vincent smirked. "The department doesn't have any sheriff's department issued cloaks of invisibility by chance?"

Silence.

"Come on. Harry Potter?" Vincent stared at us as if we were one hundred years old.

Martina smiled. "Zoey is obsessed. She loves those books."

Sarge didn't look amused. "We'll keep this quiet with or without your cloak." He eyed Martina and Vincent. "I know the two of you have plenty of experience in that department."

Ouch.

"Goodnight. Good work. Hirsch, keep me updated."

That we would do. Now to create a narrative. Why did Xavier kill Este Gomez?

24

LORI

It was positive. I know that sounds like it should be a good thing, but it wasn't. I had always envisioned I would get married one day and have children, but not at eighteen while I was finishing my first year of college. How had I let this happen? He swore he wore a condom. Not that I'd seen it, but I was sure he did. He would not have done that on purpose. How would he react when he found out the news?

Este said, "It'll be all right, Lori, we'll figure this out."

What we? Este wasn't pregnant. She hadn't made a huge mistake. I loved Freddie, and it ruined my life. "I don't know how I let this happen," I cried.

"Did you use protection?"

"Of course he did."

"Are you sure? I wouldn't exactly say he's an upstanding person." Este was never a fan of Freddie, and after he dumped me, she thought he was lower than scum at the bottom of a pond. "What do you want to do?"

Even though our mom was a single mother and her life was hard, raising two girls all by herself, she had said she loved us, and that although she hadn't planned to have children so young, it changed her life. She said we were her greatest blessings.

"I don't know what to do."

"You're so young. You have so much ahead of you. There is plenty of time to have babies, but I don't think right now is the right time."

On campus, there were booths set up with different political messaging regarding whether abortion should be legal. I always believed that a woman should have the right to choose what happened to her own body, but I had thought that I would never get an abortion. I also thought I was too smart to end up a teenage mother. Cut to being dumped and pregnant at eighteen. I had been such a fool.

There was no question about whether I could handle this on my own. I couldn't afford a full-time nanny plus college plus working and then medical school. I couldn't do it all. There was no way, unless Freddie helped. Funny. I knew better than that. The only help he had provided was helping himself out of our relationship.

Staring at the plus sign, I felt positively broken. Este took the pregnancy test out of my fingertips. "Can I throw this away? It has your pee on it."

I laughed through my tears. "Yes, please."

After she threw it away and washed her hands at the sink, she returned to me. I sat perched on the toilet, fearing that once I left that room, my entire world was going to implode. Este wrapped her arms around me and squeezed tight. "I love you, sis."

That only made me cry more.

Eventually, she released me and then stared me dead in the eyes. "You don't have to keep it."

"You don't think I should?" I asked, a little surprised.

"I think you should take your time to think about it. Think about what life would be like with a baby."

And without Freddie. She was right. I needed time to think this through and come up with a plan. I always liked having a plan. It made me feel centered when I knew what I was going to do. At that moment, I was too stunned to make a rational decision. I knew that much.

That night, I didn't sleep a wink. All I could think about was Freddie and the baby and what I would do.

At six in the morning, I forced myself to get dressed and face the day. Dressed in stretchy pants and a T-shirt, I made my way into the kitchen to get a glass of milk. Auntie was already fussing near the stove. I said, "Good morning."

"Good morning. How are you doing?"

"Okay," I lied.

"Didn't sleep well?"

"No. You can tell?" Could she tell I was different?

"You look exhausted. Maybe you should go back to bed."

"I was going to get some milk. Maybe some toast. Feeling a little hungry."

"I'm making eggs and toast. Would you like some eggs too?"

Auntie was so kind. What would she think of me if she knew the truth? What would she think if she knew I was pregnant and had a boyfriend I had kept secret? A boyfriend who dumped me with practically no explanation. I had to stop thinking about it or I would break down again. "Sure. Thanks."

"Sit down. I'll bring it over to the table."

Auntie always told her friends Este and I were such good girls. If she knew the truth about me, she wouldn't say that anymore.

Seated, I wished my situation was different. Even after a night of non-stop thinking, I wasn't sure what to do. Maybe I should tell Auntie? She was older and wiser. Maybe she could help.

She set down a plate of eggs and toast in front of me before running back with a glass of milk and then her own food. She sat down and said a quiet prayer before she ate.

My nerves got the better of me, and I decided against bringing up my predicament.

After I inhaled my food and thanked Auntie, I went into the bathroom and looked in the mirror. Auntie was right. I looked terrible, but I felt worse.

25

MARTINA

They say every picture tells a story. I hoped so. I flipped open the photo album that Mrs. Cruz set on her dining table for us to look through. We hoped these photos would tell a story about what happened the last night of their lives. It was a long shot, but it was all we had.

The cover contained paper art that read, "We love you," surrounded by pink and purple hearts. Mrs. Cruz explained the photo album was put together by Este and Lori as a gift for their mom on her last Mother's Day. They had already diagnosed her with cancer at that point.

The first page was two smiling babies with caramel colored skin and wide brown eyes and dark hair wearing nothing but a white cloth diaper. Adorable. And heartbreaking. To think about how Lori and Este started and where they ended. It didn't seem right.

I turned the page labeled Year One. It was the two girls sitting next to each other in front of a blue background, likely in a photo studio. Maybe a JC Penney store or other location at the mall where you could bring your children to have portraits taken.

On to the next, I studied the photos and was amazed to see the girls as they grew from two years to three years, and at four years, they looked like they did at eighteen. At five years, they stood tall with wide smiles and arms around each other. They wore matching birthday hats, the classic striped cones. At six, they held matching dolls while they showed smiles with missing teeth. At seven, they clutched their favorite book as shown by the caption, written in marker. At eight years old, they wore matching Care Bear costumes while holding a Jack o' lantern style trick-or-treat bucket. One of them had a rainbow on the belly and the other a shining, smiley sun.

What a lovely gift to give their mother. Would Zoey think of doing something like this for me one day? Or should I put something together? I liked to snap pictures, but I wasn't exactly the scrapbooking type. Efforts to fill her baby book ended around year three. Jared and I had filled it in diligently, but as the years went on, we had our hands full with a toddler and our jobs. After Jared, I didn't take many pictures. That needed to change.

Seeing this work of art, I knew I needed to do the same for Zoey. She was ten years old, and I tried not to think of her at eighteen when she was on her own and free to make mistakes that could alter her path and derail her life. Considering Lori had picked the wrong boy in her first year of college and it likely ended her life, I prayed for Zoey and all the other young women, that they would avoid that fate.

Turning the page, I put my hand on my chest. At age nine, the girls wore matching white coats and had stethoscopes around their necks. The caption at the bottom read, "the future Dr. Loretta Gomez and Dr. Esther Gomez."

Este and Lori didn't get to go to medical school to become doctors like they wanted to since they were nine year olds. It wasn't fair. Fighting tears, I knew we needed to find something to put Xavier and his unidentified accomplice behind bars for the rest of their lives.

At age ten, the girls held orange tabby cats. At the bottom, I learned the cats' names were Butterscotch and Maple. I turned the page as my heart grew heavier. At eleven, with missing incisors and a look as if they had done their own hairstyles. A bit messy, but the look of pride told the story. By age twelve, they were fully preteen with hands on their hips and an air of confidence.

With two and half years before my girl was a teen, others had warned me to enjoy the few years we had left.

Next page was thirteen. The girls wore red lipstick and stylish outfits. Age fourteen made me smile. One of them lay on their belly reading a book but peering at the camera, and the other held a microscope in her hand. Future scientists and doctors.

The girls had big dreams.

Fifteen looked like a prom or semi-formal dance or, most likely, their quinceañera. They both wore ball gowns that reached the floor. One was green, the other a royal blue and adorned with sparkles. They had their long, dark hair pulled back with a bit more makeup than the year before.

At sixteen, they held up a set of keys as they sat in a vehicle. The caption read, "Twins on wheels."

The last photo was of the two girls with their mother. The mother was clearly wearing a hospital gown and her girls were on either side. The bottom caption read, "We love you, Mom."

And that got me. Tears welled up, and I sniffed. "Are you okay?" Mrs. Cruz asked.

No, I wasn't okay. These beautiful young women had been missing and murdered. There had been no press. No investigation. There had been no one looking for them. It was horrific.

Wiping my eyes, I said, "I'm fine. It's heartbreaking."

Mrs. Cruz smiled, sadly. "Yes, it is. Lori and Este are lucky the two of you came across their case. You both obviously care. Unlike that man who took the missing persons report."

Hirsch and I exchanged glances. We had told Mrs. Cruz we were coming over for the photo album and to provide an update on the case. We hadn't yet told her we identified one killer. Hirsch said, "We're just sorry we didn't find it earlier."

The next page made my heart rate speed up. Hirsch put a finger on the page. "The red scarf."

It was a photo of the sisters wearing matching red scarves.

Mrs. Cruz said, "Oh, yes. I gave those to the girls for Christmas. That is the beginning of the photos from their last night."

"This was what they were wearing the last time you saw them?"

"Yes."

"Did you find either scarf when you packed up their things?"

"I don't remember. But it's been so long. We can look."

We finished a quick perusal of the remaining photos, all of Este and Lori posing wearing the scarves. Lori wore a red dress, and Este wore denim and a T-shirt. Este's clothing in the photo was a match for the items found with her remains. They did not find Lori with the scarf. If it was in the house, it would tell us Lori had come back before she died. If not, it was, in fact, her last night alive. "Yes, that would be helpful."

She led us back to their room and in front of the closet. "This box has most things that were in their drawers and their dressers — pants, socks, that kind of thing, but I never moved their coats or dresses. Lori wore a lot of dresses. Este was a jeans gal. Casual, never trying to be flashy."

Mrs. Cruz, Hirsch, and I searched the closet and boxes for the red scarf. We came up empty-handed. Mrs. Cruz said, "Well, no scarf. Is that significant?"

I said, "It is."

"Oh?"

Nodding at Hirsch, I said, "They found Este with the red scarf. Lori wasn't with hers."

"I don't understand the significance."

"First, it means there could be more evidence out there. But also, the scarf found with Este has identified a suspect."

Mrs. Cruz clutched her chest. "A suspect? The person who killed them?"

"Yes."

"Have you arrested him?" Mrs. Cruz asked.

"Not yet. We don't think he acted alone. We're trying to find more evidence to piece together what happened that night. But I promise you, the person who killed Este will go to jail."

"Who was it?"

"Unfortunately, we can't disclose that yet. It's incredibly sensitive, so we need to ask you not to share this information."

"But you'll get him and put him in jail, right?"

"Absolutely."

Mrs. Cruz said something in Spanish I didn't understand and then said, "I'm just sorry I couldn't protect them. I feel like I failed their mother."

With my hand on her shoulder, I said, "I'm sure their mother and the girls were very grateful for everything you gave them. What happened to them is not your fault. There was nothing you could have done differently that would have changed what happened."

It was Paul Xavier and Lori's boyfriend who were to blame. And I couldn't wait for Hirsch to lock them up for good.

Mrs. Cruz said, "You're kind. They were such wonderful girls."

I had no doubt about that. Unfortunately, one or both of them trusted the wrong person. And I couldn't wait to see the look on Paul Xavier's face when Hirsch slapped those cuffs on his wrists. I hoped the day arrived soon because we knew he was guilty. We just had to make sure everybody else understood that as well. We didn't want him trying to argue there was a mistake in the lab or that we had the wrong guy, trying to use his connections to get out of the charges. When we locked him up, it would be for good.

26

HIRSCH

The day was almost over, and I couldn't wait to get home to Kim. The day had been eventful, so I'd had little time to think about her, but it was hard not to, considering. Before I could think about saying goodnight to my colleagues, Jayda and Ross approached as we walked toward the squad room. "Hey, do you have a minute? I know it's the end of the day, but we received some information from Vincent, and he said I should show it to the two of you right away."

Great. All we needed was another crisis. "All right, let's talk in the squad room."

Once inside, we were the only ones present. I leaned against the wall. Jayda said, "Okay, so here's the deal. I'm not sure the significance, but when Vincent gave it to us, he was really excited and said to bring it to you right away."

"Okay, let's hear it."

"We're getting some of the background information on Richard Whitlock. The man killed ten years ago at the park in Dublin. The original file said they couldn't find a motive or anybody who would want to hurt him, so they assumed robbery, but we all know that makes little sense. Well, what we found in the background was that he worked for a financial firm, and Richard Whitlock had been extorting money from the company."

"And we think somebody from the firm murdered him because he was embezzling from his company?"

Jayda said, "Maybe."

"How much did he steal?"

"The article said eight million."

Martina said, "That sounds like eight million reasons to kill someone."

"I agree." I wasn't sure why Vincent thought we needed to see this right away.

Jayda eyed us. "You don't seem wowed by this information."

"It's good information. But I'm not sure why Vincent would want us to see it. Where did Whitlock work?"

"Richard Whitlock worked for an investment firm, Xavier and Sons."

My eyes widened, and I glanced at Martina, who looked as interested as I was.

"Have we wowed you yet?" Ross asked.

"We're wowed. We're familiar with the Xavier family."

You could have knocked me over with a feather. I waved them away from the door and brought them to the far side of the room and sat them down. Turning to Martina, I said, "We need to tell them."

Martina said, "I agree. They can be trusted."

Confusion crept across Jayda's and Ross's faces. "What is it?" Ross asked.

"We've been working a case — below the radar. A double murder. It was originally listed as a missing persons case. Twin sisters Lori and Este Gomez went missing twenty years ago. We have found their remains. It's now a homicide. David Xavier filed the report."

"A cover-up?" Jayda deduced.

"More than that. We got DNA back on one of the bodies. Paul Xavier's blood was on Este's remains."

Ross removed his ball cap and scratched the back of his head. "I was not expecting that."

Martina explained, "And here's the thing. We know Paul Xavier killed Este, but we're trying to come up with a motive. One girl was pregnant, but Xavier is not the father."

Jayda said, "A pervert? His family is clearly into some bad stuff."

I said, "No sexual assault."

Ross said, "He was helping a friend. You find the father of the baby and you find the friend. It would be a good friend or relative."

Martina wore a smug grin. "That's exactly what I said. And guess what?"

"There's more?" Jayda asked.

"Vincent found in the background checks that Sheriff Lafontaine and Paul Xavier have been best friends since high school."

Jayda's mouth dropped open.

Ross said, "Dang. So, you think Lafontaine's involved or he covered it up?"

I said, "We don't have any evidence linking Lafontaine. That's why we've been keeping it quiet."

Before I could finish my thought, Martina said, "He helped cover it up."

"The Gomez sisters?" I asked, surprised by her declaration.

"No. Yes. Probably. No, what I meant was he helped cover up the Whitlock murder. Think about it. He didn't want us working the case, and Sarge hadn't told him about it. But he knew a lot of details. He didn't want us working it because he was covering for Xavier."

Digesting Martina's accusation, I had to agree with her. It had been strange that Lafontaine knew about the Whitlock case, and the fact he didn't want us to work it meant he probably didn't realize Jayda and Ross were already working it. He was covering for his friend. His friend who was a killer.

"So, the two of you are planning on taking down the sheriff and the mayor?" she asked with wide eyes.

"That depends on what the evidence tells us. Right now, we need to put all the pieces together. We have no evidence Lafontaine covered up anything. But this is pretty damning. I need to talk to Sarge."

"Sarge knows about all this, too?"

"He does. We have to keep this within our squad. The ramifications could shut the case and the squad down."

Jayda raised her brows. "Either way, it could take us down."

I wished Jayda were wrong.

"What do you mean?" Martina asked.

"C'mon. We prove the sheriff is covering up cases and killing people plus that case you found a while back that proved the department covered up a serial killer — it might be enough for a new sheriff to come in and divert resources to clean up the department and root out bad apples. They say no press is bad press, but in this case, it's bad press. And a major PR issue for the county."

She was right. In our pursuit of justice, we could get ourselves shut down. If that was the case, so be it. It was what we signed up for. There were other departments and other jobs.

After a few choice words, I left the group and headed toward Sarge's office. The light was off. Sarge must have already gone home. It was Friday night, and I longed to do the same. But unfortunately, this couldn't wait. I pulled out my phone and dialed. The call went straight to voicemail. Maybe Sarge was on a date with Betty.

Back in the Cold Case Squad Room, I said, "Sarge isn't in his office, and he's not answering his phone. Keep this between us. Say nothing to anyone and hold tight until I talk to Sarge. And have a good weekend."

"You too, Hirsch."

I let out a breath as I packed up my things.

Martina said, "Try to have a good night, Hirsch. We'll get this figured out."

"You're right, we will. Have fun at movie night. Did you already order the pizza?"

"I'll order it when I get home. It's pretty quick. And we have ice cream left over from yesterday, so I'm set."

"All right, see you Monday."

She waved. Part of me was relieved that Sarge wasn't in his office, which meant I could go home and enjoy an evening with my wife. Even so, I wanted to know the truth, and I wanted Xavier and his pals to pay for what they did, not only to Lori and Este Gomez, but it sounded like to Richard Whitlock, too.

27

MARTINA

Frustrated, I drove home wishing we had a better understanding of what happened the night Este and Lori were killed so we could arrest Paul Xavier and lock him up. I understood we needed to have all the pieces in place to arrest him, but if it were up to me, I would have arrested him the day we found his DNA on Este's scarf. We could figure it out later, right? I had never understood politics, but I understood trying to take down Lafontaine in the process. He had to be covering up for his friend. My only question was, was that all he did? My gut was telling me Lafontaine knew what his buddy had been up to then and present day. Maybe Lafontaine didn't cover it up, or at least not initially. But he had to know about the connection to Richard Whitlock, that I was sure of. I could feel it. Lafontaine was dirty.

As I approached my house, I slowed the car before pulling into the driveway. There was an extra sedan parked at my house. No wonder Hirsch couldn't reach Sarge. He was at my house.

Parked in the driveway, I turned off the engine and called Hirsch.

"Martina, what's up?"

"Sarge is at my house."

"Really?"

It wasn't that surprising. Although Mom did usually tell me if she was having guests over. "Well, I'm guessing he's on a date with Mom or here to pick her up to take her out."

"He needs to know what's going on, Martina."

"I agree. Do you want to come over and talk to him together? There will be pizza and ice cream."

He hesitated and covered up the phone, probably speaking with Kim. It was a Friday night, and they were newlyweds. They probably had some romantic evening planned, or at least plans that included just the two of them.

"I'll come over."

"If you want to bring Kim, we can make a night of it. Zoey will be thrilled."

After Sarge had suspended me, I wanted to kick myself for introducing him to my mom. But in this situation, I would use it to benefit the team.

"Hold on." He came back on. "Kim said she'd be happy to come over, too."

"We'll see you soon."

I did not know when I joined the Cold Case Squad that work would be so intertwined with my personal life. It was like I received a bunch of new family members. There was no getting away from these folks, or was there? I couldn't help but think about what Jayda said about the fate of the squad. Admittedly, I was up to my limit with Lafontaine and his politics and was preparing myself for an exit at the end of the year, but if he was gone, I'd reconsider. But what if there was no more squad like Jayda suggested? My life and family would change once again. They say the only constant is change. Whoever *they* is.

Despite how taking down Lafontaine could affect the

squad, we had to do it. Unfortunately, my gut said that was inevitable. Lafontaine wouldn't make it through another election, whether or not we could prove he was guilty. The press would have a field day when his best friend was charged with murder. I'd be lying if I said the thought did not bring a smile to my lips.

Backpack on my shoulder, I approached the front door to my house, knowing that the days of Zoey waiting for me and hearing the pattering of her feet toward the door to let me in were long gone. Key in the door, barking sounded. And I thought, at least Barney still greeted me. I let myself in, and I heard laughter from the kitchen. After a few scratches behind Barney's ears, I snuck into my bedroom, dropped my backpack, and put away my firearm in the lockbox in my closet. With Barney, the most loyal fifteen pounds of fluff, on my heels, I strolled down the hallway into the kitchen. "Hey, everyone."

"Hey, Martina."

Zoey gave me an obligatory hug. "Hi, Mom."

With Zoey's attention diverted to Barney, I said, "Hey, Sarge. How's it going?"

"All right."

"In the house, we call him Ted, remember?"

Mom's rules.

"Ted, how's it going?" I asked, like a petulant child.

He knew better than to respond. I said, "Hey, I invited Hirsch and Kim over to enjoy movie night with us. You two ought to stick around."

"Yes! I haven't seen Auntie Kim in forever." Zoey exaggerated. It had been a few weeks, max.

I eyed Sarge. He said, "Really?"

"Yeah, really, and I know we're breaking some rules here, but we need to talk to you about something."

"Martina!" Mom protested.

"Mom, it won't take long, but it's important. Hirsch has been trying to call you."

"We don't talk shop at home. You know the rule."

Staring at her, I said, "Mom, this isn't just any other case. This is important and sensitive."

"There's something new?" Sarge asked.

"Yes."

He shook his head. "All right, well, right now, I wish I had a beer."

Mom said, "Sorry, honey."

Mom and I were both recovering alcoholics, sober a few years, but we didn't keep beer or other alcohol in the house except for parties when we had guests who enjoyed libations. "Well, I'll put that pizza order in," Mom said, displeased about the change in Friday night plans.

Looking at my girl, I saw more of her dad in her every day. Her blue eyes were Jared's, but her dark hair was mine. She was getting tall too, either from me or him. I was no shorty at five feet seven inches, but Jared hit over six feet. I wrapped my arms around her again and squeezed. "Mom, what was that for?"

"Because I'm your mom and I get to." I never wanted to let her go. But the knock on the door triggered Barney's alarm system. He yapped at the door. "That must be Hirsch and Kim."

I picked up Barney and opened the door to the picture-perfect couple. Hirsch with his dark-blond hair and bright eyes that matched Kim's. "Hey." After I gave Kim a one-armed hug, I said, "It's so good to see you. You look like you're glowing, Kim."

She blushed. "Thank you. It's good to see you too."

Zoey pushed her way through and wrapped her arms around Kim. It used to make me jealous, but I'd eventually accepted it. There would be many people who would enter Zoey's life, and Kim was easy to accept.

I led them to the kitchen, where they said hello to Mom and

Sarge. I said, "Okay. Sarge, Hirsch, and I will step out into the back yard and have a quick chat."

Mom gave me a disapproving look.

"Just this once, Mom."

"Okay," she said, as if she didn't believe me. She had to have known when she started dating Sarge that work would come up occasionally. If she knew the magnitude of this particular case, she wouldn't give me so much grief.

Outside, Sarge looked at Hirsch and then at me. "Okay, what's going on?"

Hirsch explained the latest development. Sarge looked disturbed by the idea that we were getting closer to proving Lafontaine was covering up the Whitlock murder. He shook his head. "It's compelling. And I agree it sounds like Lafontaine had to have known Xavier was involved with the Whitlock murder. But we still don't have physical evidence the sheriff has covered anything up. And he wasn't on the force when the Gomez sisters went missing, so he wasn't involved with that cover-up."

He was acting like Lafontaine was innocent. He wasn't. "So, then we can just go arrest Xavier and we're not worried about Lafontaine?" I asked, as politely as I could. Which, I admit, wasn't very.

"I think we want to find a motive first. Let's paint a picture."

My patience was growing thin. "We're going to continue to let a murderer be free until we can figure out why he did it? What if we never know why? We have his DNA at the scene. Can't we bring him in and interrogate him? Maybe he'll roll over on whoever he was helping or tell us if he had an accomplice."

Hirsch said, "At the very least, it's too close to bring in the sheriff on this. He is good friends with Paul Xavier. We have evidence of that. Do we go to IA?"

"No, don't get IA involved. I don't trust them not to go to the sheriff. It could be bad. We need to know at what level Lafontaine is involved. We need to get proof of any kind of involvement in order to piece together a picture of why Lafontaine needs to be sidelined on this one. And I agree with you that Xavier can't be free indefinitely. He's already had an extra twenty years." Sarge looked at me. "Maybe Martina is right. Maybe we bring Xavier in."

"But as soon as we get a warrant, Lafontaine will know."

"That is true. We have to get it quietly from a judge we can trust to keep it quiet."

"You know anyone?" Hirsch asked.

"Let me make a call. We'll come up with a plan. I don't like dirty cops any more than you, Hirsch. Now, let's eat some pizza. We'll regroup after."

We reentered the home more relaxed. Zoey and Kim were gabbing on the couch while Mom stood at the entrance to the kitchen. Sarge approached her and gave her a light peck on the cheek and whispered something. It was sweet and disturbing at the same time.

The doorbell rang. "That must be the pizza."

Sarge said, "I'll get it," and hurried down the hall with Barney in tow.

Mom said to Kim and Hirsch, "Sorry, I don't have any beer or wine for you to enjoy with your pizza. But we didn't know you were coming over." She eyed me with a little contempt. Mom liked to be the hostess with the mostest.

Kim waved her off. "Oh, don't worry, I'm not drinking, anyway."

The room silenced. I said, "You're not?"

Kim turned dark crimson. "No, I'm not."

I looked over at Hirsch, who was trying to suppress the

smile that was forming on his face. "What?" I asked with delight.

Kim nodded as teardrops formed in her eyes.

I said, "Oh my gosh! You're having a baby! Congratulations!" I gave Kim a hug and then Hirsch. "Well, now I know you're good at keeping secrets," I teased.

Kim said, "We weren't telling anybody yet. It's still pretty early."

Zoey moved in to give Kim a hug. "You're having a baby. Do you know if it's a boy or girl?"

"Not yet. It's too early for that."

Mom said, "Well, now we have to celebrate."

Sarge walked in with two pizza boxes. "What did I miss?"

Hirsch cleared his throat. "Kim is pregnant. We're having a baby."

Sarge said, "Finally, some good news around here." He smiled. "Congratulations to both of you."

Hirsch thanked him. I smiled wide, so happy for Hirsch and Kim. A baby. It had been years since I'd held a tiny infant in my arms. Finally, some good news, indeed.

28

LORI

Unsure what I was going to do about the baby, I knew I needed answers. Freddie and my relationship ended so abruptly, with no explanation, but I needed an explanation. Would it make a difference? I didn't know. But he and I needed to have an honest conversation about where we stood and what went wrong. Not that it meant we would get back together, but I needed to know if it was all an illusion. Would it make a difference in my decision about the baby? Maybe. Maybe not. Mustering all my courage, I dialed his number. "Hey."

"What's up? Why are you calling?"

Not the, "I miss you," I was hoping for. "I just wanted to have a conversation. Why did you break up with me? I need to know. Was our entire relationship and love a lie?"

After several seconds, he said, "It wasn't a lie. It just couldn't work."

Did he sound sad? "Why?"

"Look, there was a reason I didn't introduce you to my friends and family. They didn't know about you, at first. When we wanted to use the cabin, my mother wanted to know why, and then I told her about you."

He had kept me a secret? Why? "So, if we hadn't made plans to go to the cabin, they wouldn't have ever known about me?"

"It's complicated."

Shaking my head, I was more confused than before. "How?"

"Look, I'm not proud of this, but when I told my mother your name, she figured out you're Mexican."

"I'm not Mexican. My family is from Honduras. I'm from New Orleans."

"You know what I mean."

"It's a different country." Was he really that ignorant?

"Okay. Well, it doesn't matter. My family won't allow it."

Not allow what? For him to date a person from Honduras? Or Mexico? Because of the color of my skin? They didn't even know me. I was going to be a doctor. "So, you broke up with me because your family doesn't approve."

"Yes."

Too stunned to speak, I waited.

He said, "You don't understand what it's like."

"I guess not." My baby's family was racist. Suddenly, all the secrecy and 'staying in our bubble' made sense. Why he blew up when I mentioned marriage. He knew his family would never approve. He knew we didn't have a future together. It had been a lie. All of it. There was no way he actually loved me and also would break up with me because his family didn't approve. Those two conditions couldn't exist at the same time. He was weak. And spoiled. And selfish. And I was having his child. Would it have been better to not have known the truth?

How would he respond to the news that I was pregnant? I had a guess. And I didn't like it.

"I'm really sorry. You're a great girl and so smart. You'll forget about me in no time. I'm sure of it."

Maybe that would be true if I wasn't pregnant with his baby. "I have to go."

"Take care."

I was too disgusted with him to say another word. How had I been so stupid? How had I fallen so hard for an illusion? Because he knew what to say and when to say it to get what he wanted. I was a fool. When it seemed too good to be true, it probably was. Defeated, I slunk back to Este and my room.

Este was lying on her bed reading our biology text book. She glanced up. "Hey."

"Hey."

"Did you tell him?"

Not sure when I would've slipped it in. I guess I could have said, "Oh your family doesn't like Latinas. Well, guess what? I've got a little one with your last name brewing inside me." No, I had to be sure what I was going to do before I told him.

"No. I chickened out." I plopped onto my bed. "What am I going to do?"

"Whatever you decide. I'm team Lori."

"Thanks." That made exactly two people on my team.

"You know you have to tell him, eventually."

"I know. But not today." With that, I lay on my side and cried until I couldn't cry any more.

29

MARTINA

The scent of Vincent's bacon and cheese croissant invaded my space. It smelled rich and salty as opposed to the healthy bowl of yogurt with berries and almonds I had for breakfast. I wanted nothing heavy, weighing me down, but that didn't mean the sandwich didn't smell heavenly. "How's the sandwich?"

Vincent nodded with his mouth full. I didn't blame him for eating in the squad room. It was Saturday morning and none of us were supposed to be there. But we needed to put together a case in order to arrest Xavier and quietly try to find evidence Lafontaine was involved. But so far, we had come up empty-handed. There was nothing linking Lafontaine to Xavier except the fact they were friends, had posed for photos in the newspaper, and their school records. It was enough of a connection to keep Lafontaine out of the loop while still keeping our jobs. If I didn't know better, I could think maybe Lafontaine had covered up his friend's crimes, not realizing Xavier's involvement or that Xavier had said to keep the cases buried without explaining he was actually guilty of a crime. Not exactly on the up and up, but not covering up a murder, either.

But I knew better.

Lafontaine worked in various departments throughout the county before landing himself in the sheriff's seat. I had always wondered how he had gotten the position being as young as he was. Not that he was a spring chicken at forty-two years old, but he'd been the sheriff for five years. His family and political connections to the Xaviers explained how he'd taken the sheriff's seat at thirty-six.

My gut said he was dirty.

Rereading the Whitlock file, I concluded a cover-up wasn't obvious and it would be difficult to prove one had taken place. There wasn't a thorough investigation, but they had questioned neighbors and collected the physical evidence on the body and surrounding area. The original investigators assumed the blood on Whitlock's clothing was his, so forensics hadn't been done. The lack of testing could produce a little side-eye, but considering the forensic testing Jayda and Ross submitted confirmed the only blood on Richard Whitlock's clothing was his own, it was weak.

Vincent had theorized Whitlock's murder was a professional hit, likely hired by the Xaviers' firm Whitlock had been embezzling from. A theory. Not proof. And it was a big if, considering the team had found no evidence that Whitlock had taken the eight million dollars. If he had, he had hidden it well. The money hadn't shown up in his financials or in his wife's or any of his family member's names. The only explanation was that he put the money in an offshore account in Switzerland or somewhere in the Caribbean, where they didn't provide that information to the United States. Or he hadn't taken the eight million and someone at the firm used him as a scapegoat for someone else's thievery.

Maybe my personal feelings against Lafontaine were clouding my judgement. Maybe he wasn't involved. Just because his best friend got away with murder twenty years ago and maybe ten years ago didn't mean he was mixed up in it.

But... birds of a feather flock together? One's a killer, and one's the sheriff. Opposites attract?

I was exhausted by assumptions. I wanted facts.

Staring down at the girls' autopsies and the findings from the forensics team, I wanted answers.

Why had Xavier killed Este Gomez?

Had he killed Lori too? And Richard Whitlock?

Hirsch shut the lid to his laptop. "I'm not finding anything."

"I haven't either. Maybe we're looking at this wrong."

Vincent said, "We have zero evidence Lafontaine covered up anything. Maybe he didn't. We need to find who did."

"Okay, so we search for any similarities between responding officers and who worked the cases?"

"That's easy on the Gomez case. It was David Xavier who took the missing persons report, and he didn't enter their information in the missing persons database. Is his name anywhere near the Whitlock case?" Hirsch asked.

Vincent shook his head and finished chewing his delicious smelling sandwich. "No. No Xaviers near the Whitlock case except the fact that he worked for the Xaviers."

"What if Lafontaine wasn't covering up for Xavier, initially? Maybe it's an after-the-fact cover-up. He's friends with Xavier, so he just happens to know about the cases?"

It felt like we were going in circles. We needed to arrest Xavier and put the screws to him.

Hirsch seemed to contemplate that scenario. "It's possible. Xavier's crimes were committed before Lafontaine had any actual power within the department. He is aware of them and he's just suppressing them, which is the same as a cover-up."

"Someone could simply ask Lafontaine how he knew about the Whitlock case?"

Vincent and I both stared at Hirsch.

Hirsch shook his head. "Not going to happen. This team is skating on thin ice as it is. And I can't start interrogating Lafontaine about why he doesn't want us working on a specific case. I don't think that's a good move at all."

"What if Sarge brought it up casually? Or brought up that it was still being investigated and see what his reaction is?" I offered.

Hirsch leaned back in his chair and crossed his arms across his chest. "I would prefer we don't go to Lafontaine for anything. We have two cases we're working in secret."

It was a good point.

Vincent crinkled up the wrapper from his sandwich. "Or maybe we're thinking about this backward. Maybe it's not Lafontaine covering up for Xavier. Xavier's covering for Lafontaine."

Xavier had the political power from birth, not Lafontaine. He didn't get the politics edge until he befriended Xavier. "That's an interesting angle. So, maybe Lafontaine was involved in the Gomez murders and Xavier helped him out. He says hey Lafontaine, don't worry about it. I've got family in the department. We'll make sure this never comes back to us."

Hirsch's eyes grew larger. "Now you're saying that Lafontaine's a murderer?"

Vincent shot the balled-up wrapper across the room and straight into the wastebasket. "Nothing but net." Hirsch and I stared at him. Vincent said, "Lafontaine could be a killer. Xavier's a killer. Why not?"

I added, "Killers look just like you and me. They're not all big, bad, scary wolves in grandma's clothing."

Hirsch looked unconvinced that his boss was a murderer. Well, then he was going to have to disprove the theory. "So, if we run with this killer sheriff idea, what's next?" he asked.

"We get Lafontaine's DNA."

Vincent said, "Not it."

I couldn't help but laugh. "Not it."

Vincent and I continued to laugh as Hirsch rolled his eyes. "I'll talk to Sarge to see what we can do."

I thought back to my time in the sheriff's office. He had a large executive desk and on the right-hand corner with a mug of coffee next to a framed photo of his family. "Maybe Sarge can swipe his favorite coffee mug."

Hirsch said, "It won't hold up in court."

"It doesn't have to. We're just exploring at this point. If it excludes him, we're done. If we need DNA for the prosecution, we should have enough for a warrant because we'll come up with a good enough story."

"I'll talk to Sarge and take a peek into Lafontaine's office."

"Good plan," Vincent added.

Hirsch said, "So, we're done here." As if he couldn't wait for this to be over. I got the vibe Hirsch didn't think Lafontaine killed anyone, and he thought this avenue was a waste of time. But ignoring the possibility would be foolish.

"Hey, are you going to share the news?" I said, trying to lighten the mood.

Hirsch's demeanor changed. He smiled. "Kim is pregnant. She's only twelve weeks, so we haven't made an announcement yet."

"Congratulations, man. That's so awesome."

"It is. It's awesome. It's terrifying. It's all those things."

I quipped, "You sound like a parent already."

30

HIRSCH

Standing in the corner of the conference room, I said, "Thanks, Sarge."

"This never happened."

Martina slipped her backpack strap over her shoulder. "Never happened. Let's go, Hirsch."

"Thanks again, Sarge."

He waved us off like he couldn't wait for this investigation to be over. He and I both. After this, the skies would open up and life would change. I wasn't sure I was ready for it.

We headed down the hallway with precious cargo in Martina's backpack. It could be the piece of evidence that exonerated Lafontaine or put him smack in the middle of the Gomez murder investigation. If Lafontaine wasn't involved, we would have to pull the trigger on the arrest of Xavier.

We had found zero physical evidence Lafontaine covered anything up. It may have been all David Xavier, Paul's cousin. Once we arrested Paul, we'd bring in David at the same time to ensure he didn't run. The arrest warrant was requested and approved. All we needed was the green light from Sarge to serve it. I didn't blame him for the delay. It was going to be tricky considering the second we arrested Xavier, the sheriff was likely to realize what we had been doing behind his back. And he was going to be flaming mad. Sarge said he wanted to be careful so that we all had jobs at the end of the day.

Martina seemed gung-ho to take down Lafontaine, but I wasn't convinced. He was vain and mostly concerned with his standing in the community, but I didn't make him for a killer. Hopefully, his DNA could be pulled from the mug Sarge had swiped from his office earlier that day. Sarge explained he offered to get him a refill of coffee in order to swap it with an identical mug from the cupboard while covertly putting the mug from the sheriff in a brown paper bag. The sheriff would never know. And we would never speak of it.

I held my breath as we walked toward the sheriff's office. Hopefully, he didn't spot Martina and me as we made our way to Kiki's lab to hand off the evidence.

No luck.

"Hi, Detective Hirsch," he said with a smile, obviously making a point to ignore Martina once again. It was rude and childish, but not indicative of a killer.

Hoping he didn't see the sweat forming on my brow, I said, "Happy Monday, Sheriff."

He eyed Martina. "Happy Monday to you too. How is the Ackerman case going? Any fresh developments?"

"We're still going through the case files. It looks like they did a pretty good job investigating the first time, but they didn't identify any actual suspects. We're starting there. We think there is a chance we have interviewed the person who took Gerald. Don't worry, we won't let you down. We will find Gerald Ackerman."

He glanced over at Martina and then back at me. "Where are the two of you headed?"

"To see Dr. Scribner."

"Why would you be visiting the medical examiner if you're looking for suspects on the Ackerman boy?"

Okay. He was petty, childish, and a jerk who was trying to dictate how we did the job. But he was also astute.

"When you handed us the Ackerman file, I reached out to her to see if she had any ten-year-old John Does come across her desk or any of her colleagues. She recalled a case that happened in Portland. She says there was a ten-year-old boy found dead in the crawl space of a suspected sex offender. We're going to see if the remains could be Gerald Ackerman." I hoped that was believable because I didn't want him to know we were going to the forensics lab. There were no forensics associated with the Ackerman abduction.

"Wow, that would be a quick win for the two of you," he said with a smirk.

Was it progress that he was acknowledging Martina?

"We have our fingers and toes crossed, sir."

"Okay, then, I'll leave you to it."

We continued on, and I could feel my pits were wet. Nerves while taking down a suspect was one thing, but lying straight to the sheriff's face was not something I could get used to. We sailed past the forensics lab, as if we were, in fact, going to see Dr. Scribner. At that point, I couldn't put anything past the sheriff. Would he call Dr. Scribner to see if we had been there? Maybe. I mean, he could be completely innocent or the guiltiest of guilty and there was only one way we would find out.

We went into Dr. Scribner's office. "Hi, Dr. Scribner."

"Hi. I didn't know you were coming by."

"We have to admit, this is a bit of a decoy." I explained the situation and what I had told the sheriff.

Dr. Scribner nodded and looked behind us. "Your secret is safe with me. Coast is clear."

"It's much appreciated."

"Good luck, you two."

We headed back down the hall toward the forensics lab. We hadn't told Kiki we were coming, so I had to wave outside the lab, where she was wearing a lab coat and safety goggles. It was the first time I had seen her in the lab. Glancing back past Martina, I had to make sure the sheriff had not been following us. This covert investigation was making me paranoid, and I couldn't wait for it to be over. I wanted to be home on the weekends and weeknights to spend time with my wife and our bean. Kim was already talking about which room to turn into a nursery and what colors to paint the walls. Her excitement was beautiful, and I wanted to be with her every step of the way.

Kiki pointed toward her office and started walking that direction. We continued down the hallway and turned to the office area for the lab workers. We walked into her office and waited. She arrived, still wearing her lab coat. "This is a surprise."

"We have something we need to have tested for DNA."

"Is it for the special case?"

Martina nodded. "It's a coffee cup. We hope there is enough material on it for DNA testing." Martina fished out the brown paper bag with the mug from her backpack.

"May I ask who it belongs to?" Kiki asked, obviously curious.

"It's better you don't know."

She gave a knowing smile. "Understood. It's perfect timing. I was just preparing samples for the remaining forensic evidence from Este Gomez. If this is related to that, we'll get a hit."

I nodded.

"Any idea when we'll get the results?" Martina asked.

"I'm hoping a few days tops. I already prepped the samples. I'll rush it."

"Thank you."

"I'll stop by as soon as I have the results."

The look Kiki gave us made me think she knew exactly where we had retrieved the evidence.

As we headed back to the squad room, Martina said, "You know, I think you could do undercover work."

"No, thank you."

"That's true. You're a family man now."

Martina was loving the fact that I was going to become a father. And so was I. I had wondered if I would ever be a parent or find the right partner. Fatherhood scared me more than anything had scared me before. I would be responsible for protecting Kim and our child. With so many terrible people in this world who did terrible things, I would have to make sure none of those monsters got anywhere near my family.

At the end of the hall, I spotted Vincent speaking to a woman wearing a dark blue suit. Her hair was pinned back in a bun, and she was laughing at something Vincent had said. He saw the two of us and waved.

"Hey, Vincent."

"Hey, boss. Hey, Martina. This is Agent Jessica Holley with the FBI profiler program. She was just coming by to get a copy of the files to create her profile and recommendation."

I shook Agent Holley's hand. "It's very nice to meet you, and thank you for helping us out."

"Anything for Vinny."

Vinny? Before I could say anything, Martina said, "How do you two know each other?"

"Vincent was my college dorm RA. He let me get away with a few things back in the day. So, I owe him one."

"Or seven," Vincent added.

I said, "I can't picture you as a resident advisor." That meant that Vincent was in charge of college kids and had to ensure that everybody was doing what they were supposed to do. That didn't sound like Vincent at all. Although Agent Holley said he let her slide on a few things. That was more the Vincent I knew.

Martina said, "I can only imagine what Vincent was like back then."

"Oh, he's the same," Agent Holley said. She looked at our puzzled faces and then smiled. "When he grows on you, there's no way to wash him off."

Martina laughed at that. "Oh, that, we understand."

"Any idea when your profile will be complete?" I asked.

"Just a few days."

I said, "That's incredible. Thank you again. If there's anything we can do to help, please, let us know." I fished out a business card and handed it to her, and Martina did the same.

"Will do. Very nice meeting you."

"You, too."

At least that was one thing going the right direction. In a few days, we could have a suspect in the Gerald Ackerman case. I was starting to believe Martina, that maybe the sheriff gave that case to us because he thought it wasn't solvable. But he should know better. You give us a case, we won't stop until we solve it.

31

MARTINA

Jayda pointed at the whiteboard. "As you can see from the phone records, Whitlock called someone approximately thirty minutes before he was killed."

How had the original investigators not figured that out? Maybe Xavier had pressured the original investigator to not spend much time on it, or they had found it and were told to lose it. "Probably whoever he was supposed to meet."

"Exactly."

Glancing at my Timex, I noted we had ten minutes before our meeting with Agent Holley from the FBI's behavioral analysis unit. Her profile for Gerald Ackerman's abductor was ready. "Have you identified who the phone number is registered to?"

Jayda turned to Ross. "Would you like to do the honors?"

"Nah, I'll let you."

Patience thinning, I said, "If anybody would do the honors, I would appreciate it."

Jayda curtsied. "The person Richard Whitlock called thirty minutes before he died was our favorite murdering mayor, Paul Xavier."

No wonder they went for the theatrics. How dirty was Paul Xavier? As dirty as they come. We already had him on a double murder, and he was the last person who had spoken to another murder victim ten years later.

Who at the sheriff's department had been covering up all of Paul Xavier's crimes? Was it David Xavier? David had been retired five years, so he could have influenced the Whitlock investigation to run cold. He didn't have to have his name on a report to do that. Or had it been Lafontaine?

More terrifying than the idea that Paul Xavier had gotten away with up to three murders was the fact these were only two cases we had stumbled upon. What would happen if we did a review of every single cold case? Would we find more cover-ups?

Hirsch scratched his forehead with a pointer finger. "Well, this is some sparkly confetti at the Xavier party."

What was with the Cold Case Squad? Were they all training to start their own comedy troupe? "What's next, boss?" I asked Hirsch. If you can't beat them, join them.

Hirsch smirked. "Nice. I spoke with Sarge a few minutes ago. He's okay with us arresting Paul Xavier as soon as the rest of the forensics come back."

"Even if we haven't identified the father of Lori's baby?"

"Even if we get no further evidence, we can't let Paul Xavier remain free. Who knows what else he's done?"

Finally. "Good."

"What do you need from us, boss?" Jayda asked.

"You could write this up and start preparing interview questions. As soon as Kiki tells us she's got all the forensics testing complete, we're moving in on Xavier and bringing in David and Lafontaine for questioning too."

Ross said, "You got it."

I stood up. "Hirsch, we need to go." Looking at Jayda and

Ross, I said, "We have to meet with the FBI profiler on the Ackerman case."

"Hands full, huh?" Jayda asked.

Hirsch said, "When it rains, it pours."

"Grab your umbrella, Hirsch."

Hirsch laughed, and we headed out of the squad room. "How lucky do you think we'll get today?" he asked.

"I said a prayer on the way to the conference room."

Hirsch remained unconvinced by the power of prayer. Across the cubicle space, Vincent and Agent Holley were speaking quietly and smiling. Agent Holley again wore a dark suit with her hair pulled back in a bun, like she had a few days ago, but also with a splash of red lipstick. She was rather striking with her dark hair and olive skin. Not that it mattered. All I hoped was that she gave us a suspect because being away from your child for five years had to be excruciating. I couldn't imagine what Gerald Ackerman's parents were going through. They had moved into a nice, safe suburban neighborhood just to have their child snatched away from them in an instant. The thought of Zoey being taken was more than I could handle.

We greeted one another and headed into the conference room rather quietly. The door shut, and we all took a seat. Agent Holley opened the lid of binder number two of four for the Gerald Ackerman investigation.

"Thank you for working so quickly on this. I imagine you're very busy," Hirsch said.

"Oh yeah, they keep us plenty busy, but between everyone in this room, I'm actually on vacation this week, so I had some free time."

"Your supervisors let you work on your vacation time?" Hirsch asked.

"It's not work. It's a favor," she said with a wink.

I wasn't totally sure what that meant. We had submitted the

paperwork. Maybe after that, she convinced her supervisors she'd work it on her off time. Whatever the reason, I was grateful. "All right, what did you find?" I asked, more impatiently than I meant. But I was excited and wanted to know.

"Well, based on the age of the child, the neighborhood, and Gerald's routine, I think I have a pretty solid profile. From that, I have identified two suspects, and they are in this binder." She tapped the cover with her finger.

"That's great."

Agent Holley continued, "According to the records, Gerald rode his bike to school every day Monday through Friday. He lived four blocks from the school, which means the person who took him had little time to act. This makes me believe the abductor had been watching Gerald, or it was someone close to the Ackerman family or someone from the neighborhood or all three. I believe whoever took Gerald knew his routine in the morning, knew what time he left his house and what time he would be at the location they snatched him from."

"And that helps you?" I asked. Never having worked with a profiler before, Agent Holley's process fascinated me.

"Yes, that's only part of it. I also think the person who took Gerald owned a van or truck or a type of vehicle that would allow them to grab Gerald and throw his bike in the vehicle without it being seen."

It sickened me that someone, many someones, would steal a child. But the thought it had been planned somehow made it worse.

Hirsch and I nodded to show we were following her line of thinking.

"I also believe based on the planning that went into the abduction and subsequent acts between the perpetrator and the child, the abductor is single, lives alone, and has access to children on a daily basis. This was a pedophile."

"That's not good news."

Understatement.

"Unfortunately not. So, before getting too deep into the details of why I chose the two suspects, you'll see here that I've marked each suspect with a yellow sticky note. One is a neighbor of the Ackermans. He lives alone, owns a van, is a painter, is in his thirties, and inherited the home from his parents when they died eight years ago. He had means and opportunity. He easily could've seen Gerald driving by on his bike every single morning and planned the abduction from his living room."

"Do you know if the neighbor still lives there?"

"I haven't rechecked his status. That's Vinny's job," she said as she nudged Vincent.

Vincent, or Vinny, as Agent Holley called him, said, "I checked. Trent Blackwell still lives at the same address, and he has the same phone number."

"Sounds like we need to visit Mr. Blackwell."

Agent Holley said, "Well, while you're at it, here's the second suspect." She pulled the pages to the spot with the second yellow sticky note. "This one is the assistant coach for the local baseball team. He lived about two miles from where Gerald was abducted. However, the baseball field where he works is at the school, four blocks from Gerald's home, and it's the school that Gerald attended. In his interview statement, the assistant coach said he didn't remember Gerald. He never saw him around when he was at the field. However, the coach of the baseball team, who was also questioned, said he remembered seeing Gerald on his bike because he was friends with two members of his baseball team. So, either the assistant coach didn't notice Gerald or he was lying."

Not as compelling a suspect if you asked me.

She continued, "The assistant coach also owns a van and lives alone in an apartment two miles away."

Hirsch said, "So, we have two people to question and conduct deep dives on their backgrounds. Okay, tell us about the assistant coach, Vincent. Did you look him up?"

"I did. Marcus Feldman moved, but as you can see on the sticky note, I put his new address, phone number, and employer details there."

Agent Holley said, "Both of them fit the profile. Either could've taken Gerald."

But who was more likely? "Agent Holley, if you were betting on which guy is our guy, what would you say?"

A small smile crept onto her face, and she turned to Vincent. "How about this? I'll write it down on a piece of paper, and if I'm right, you have to buy me dinner."

Was this a romantic thing with Vincent? Did Agent Holley not realize Vincent was dating Amanda? I assumed they were still together and had been for over a year.

Vincent said, "Fair enough."

Agent Holley laughed. "I'm teasing. I would look closely at the neighbor. The baseball assistant coach may just be a creep. But the neighbor likely saw him every single day and planned the whole thing. He may not even have had to use his van because his house was so close to where Gerald was abducted. He could've picked him up and brought him back to his house. It would've been easy. I would recommend getting a warrant to search his computer, in addition to his property. I bet you will find child sex abuse materials on the computer. If he took Gerald, chances are it was something he fantasized about doing to some other child. Even by his speech patterns in his interview, the guy's no doubt a creep."

Color me impressed. "Wow. Thank you so much."

"You're very welcome. I also wrote up all my findings and

description of the profile in a report that is tucked into the binder here. I understand that this favor is on the down low."

"Lately, that's the name of the game around here."

"And here I thought cold cases were boring."

We all laughed nervously. It seemed to be the sentiment about cold cases from other members of law enforcement. But in my experience, cold cases were anything but boring.

A knock on the door made me stiffen. Hirsch hurried up, opened the door, and poked his head out. "Oh, hi. What is it?"

I couldn't tell who he was talking to and his inching out of the room made it so I could no longer hear what they were saying. He shut the door and sat back down. "I'm sorry. What were you saying?"

Agent Holley said, "Oh, I think we're all done unless anyone has questions?"

I did, but for Hirsch. Like why was he fidgeting like he couldn't wait to get out of there? "I'm good."

Vincent turned to Agent Holley. "I'll walk you out."

We thanked her as Vincent escorted her out.

"Who was that?"

Hirsch grinned. "It was Kiki. She's done with the testing."

32

LORI

Each step felt like wading through water. Life was moving forward and leaving me behind. When I thought I couldn't cry another single tear, I learned I could. With Freddie and the baby on my mind, I found it hard to focus on school. Work was a little easier since all I had to do was answer phones, clean, take orders, and bring out food to the customers. That was easy enough. Despite the passing of time, I still didn't know what to do about the baby. That wasn't totally true. In a perfect world, Freddie would run back to me, saying he had been wrong. He'd been a fool. When he learned about the baby, he'd be scared but filled with love, too. In a heartbeat, he would get down on his knee and not only beg for my forgiveness, but also my hand in marriage with a promise to raise our family together.

It was stupid. A fantasy.

As the weeks went on, I knew I was running out of time to make a decision. Or a few decisions. If I didn't keep the baby, did I still need to tell Freddie?

Ever since Mama died, the days felt like an uphill battle. Since I learned I was pregnant, that hill had turned into Mount Everest.

It was four in the afternoon, but I was exhausted from my heartbreak and the life growing inside of me. Lying in my bed, I shut my eyes, hoping it would help. If nothing else, it would use up less of my energy that had already dwindled from trying to stand or walk or pretend everything was fine to everyone except Este.

I hadn't heard a single word from Freddie since our conversation explaining his family was a bunch of racists, so he had to break up with me. What a creep, right? He should've lied. Would that be better?

There had been no phone calls telling me he missed me and that he made a big mistake. There was no grand gesture. There was no white horse with my prince atop with a wedding ring in one pocket and his heart in the other. Fairytales.

Fairytales weren't real.

My life was real. I was eighteen, pregnant, and alone. I didn't even have my mama's shoulder to cry on. I had my sister, but she was also only eighteen, as much as she said she would help so I didn't have to face this alone. But what could she do? She went to school just like I did. I hadn't had the heart to tell Auntie, knowing she would be so disappointed in me. I was disappointed in myself. How had I been so stupid to think he wanted anything other than a physical relationship with me? What signs had I missed?

My bedroom door creaked open, and I prayed it was Este and not Auntie. I couldn't pretend to be happy for another moment. I thought it might actually kill me. The door shut quietly. Slowly, I opened my eyes. "Hi."

"You know it's four in the afternoon?" Este asked, with pity in her eyes.

"I do."

"I know you're sad, but you can't just lie around all day. We have homework and you have to go to work tonight."

In my book, I had recently promoted Este to Captain Obvious. "I know. I just couldn't be up anymore. I'm only going to rest for a bit."

Every hope and every dream had crashed down to my feet. How could I fall so far from where I wanted to be? When Freddie and I were together, he said all the right things, like he was in love, like he'd never been in love before and then, boom, we're over. Not a single phone call in two weeks just to see how I'm doing. He had to know he had devastated me.

"Lori, I know you don't want to hear this, but you need to call him."

I sat up, put the pillow behind me, and leaned up against the wall. Este had been pressuring me to tell Freddie about the pregnancy, but I hadn't been able to bring myself to pick up the phone. "I don't know what to say."

"He needs to know, even if the two of you aren't together. Call him." Este sat on her bed, facing me.

"So that he can tell me he doesn't want me or the baby?"

"That's not why. Whether he wants to or not, if you keep the baby, he has to help take care of it. And if not him, his family. It's his child too. He needs to know."

I didn't know how I felt about that. I mean, yes, he was responsible as much as I was. It took two of us to get here. If that was true, why did I feel so utterly alone? But Este was right. I had to tell him. I'd just been too devastated to actually do it. Facing him — I couldn't bear it, knowing he didn't want me anymore.

Este moved over to my bed and put her hand on mine. "If it helps, I can go with you to talk to him. You don't have to do this alone."

As much as Este had always been my closest friend and confidant, her constantly reminding me I didn't have to do it alone was grating on my nerves. I was alone. No amount of words would change that. "You don't need to do that."

"When are you going to tell him?"

"I guess now is as good a time as any." I was done fighting and pretending to be strong. With his phone number permanently in my memory, I reached over to the phone and dialed. "Hello."

"Hi, Freddie. It's Lori."

"Hey. What's up?"

Hey, what's up? As if I was just some old friend he hadn't seen in a while. "I need to talk to you about something."

"What is it?"

"Not over the phone. I need to see you in person. It's important."

"You have me worried."

I said, "I miss you," and nearly kicked myself. It wasn't what I had planned to say. Why had I?

"I miss you too."

He did?

He was hot and cold and warm and freezing. His moods were dizzying.

"Oh, well, that's not why I was calling. There is something we need to discuss in person. Can we meet?" I asked, begging the universe that I would have the strength to get through this.

"When?"

"I have to be at work at five-thirty. I guess before then or maybe tomorrow?"

"I can meet you today. Maybe in the parking lot outside the restaurant. How about five?"

That was easier than I thought. I was so confused. "Okay. I'll see you in a bit."

"Bye."

I returned the receiver to the phone base.

"You told him you missed him?"

"It just came out." It had, and I wished it hadn't. But he said he missed me, too. That must mean something.

"But he's going to meet you?"

"Yeah, before work."

"You sure you don't want me to be there?"

"I am. I got myself into this and have to fix it alone."

Maybe this wasn't all doom and gloom. Maybe he realized that we were meant to be together. He might have realized that his family's demands were terrible. Maybe he realized we were destined to be. Re-energized, I knew I needed to find the perfect outfit to win him back.

WITH MY FLIRTIEST dress hugging my curves, I approached his car and knocked on the window. He leaned over to open the door, and I slid on to the passenger seat. "Hi."

"Hey."

He looked so handsome wearing that baby blue polo shirt I loved. It matched his blue eyes. Would our baby have his eyes? Until that moment, I hadn't contemplated what our baby would look like. If it came out the perfect mix of him and me, it would be a light cocoa color with bright blue eyes. Our baby would be gorgeous.

"What is it that you wanted to talk to me about?" he asked, sadly.

He must've missed me as much as I missed him. I squeezed my eyes shut. This was harder than I had expected. He put his hand on my arm, and I opened my eyes. "What is it?" he asked, fully concerned.

It was then or never. "I'm pregnant."

His eyes widened, and he turned the color of a sheet, a white one, like a ghost.

"Are you sure?"

I nodded. "Yeah, I took three tests."

"And it's mine?"

Annoyed, I said, "Of course. You're the only person I've ever been with in that way."

He seemed stunned, as if what we had done couldn't have possibly created a child.

"What do you plan to do? Are you going to keep it?"

"I don't know." I don't know why I said that. My heart knew what it wanted. It wanted Freddie and this baby. I wanted the three of us to be a family.

"Okay," he stuttered, as if he wasn't sure what else to say.

I didn't blame him, considering I still didn't know what to say, and I had known about the baby for two weeks. "I haven't made a decision yet, but I just thought you should know."

"Thank you for telling me. I need some time to digest this. Maybe we can talk more after you get off work, or another day. Whenever you are up to it. You probably need to rest, right?"

He was rightfully freaked out but was being thoughtful, too. Like the old Freddie. The one who existed before he broke my heart.

"Maybe tomorrow or something."

"After school?" he offered.

"Okay."

We made plans to see each other again to talk about our baby. He hadn't yelled or screamed, and he didn't say he didn't want us. Us. Maybe not all hope was lost. Feeling lighter, I pulled open the door to climb out when Freddie stopped me. He turned my face to meet his gaze. "I love you. I mean it."

"I love you too."

He moved in closer for a sweet kiss. I had missed the feel of his lips on mine. His arms around my body. He gave a half-grin. "I don't want to make you late for work."

Feeling tingly all over, I stepped out of the car and toward Bayou Restaurant with butterflies in my stomach, and it wasn't the baby. It was Freddie. I knew it couldn't be over between us.

33

MARTINA

Staring at Hirsch like a madwoman, I said, "Well, what are we waiting for?"

He grabbed the Gerald Ackerman binder and said, "Nothing now. Let's go. Kiki said she'd wait for us in the squad room."

On our way to the squad room, Vincent ran up next to us. "What's up?"

"Kiki's done with her testing."

Vincent whistled. "Woohoo. Big day."

"Keep it down."

Vincent quieted and opened the door. "After you."

Hirsch and I hurried inside. A quick scan revealed only Jayda, Ross, and Kiki were in the room, speaking animatedly about something.

Jayda looked over and waved at us. "We're just going over the forensics from the Richard Whitlock murder."

"Anything new?"

"No."

Kiki said, "My team finished testing the soil and a cigarette butt near the scene. Saliva from the cigarette is a match for

Whitlock. The soil had blood droplets in it that were a match for Whitlock, but nothing out of the ordinary that would lead us to a suspect."

As much as I cared about all of our cases, I was more than a little eager to hear about the forensics on the Gomez case.

"We still think it was a professional hit, right?" Hirsch asked.

"We do, but Kiki's team has finished the testing. The only way we'll break the case is if we can find a paper trail for a murder-for-hire transaction, a witness steps forward, or we can get a confession from our favorite politician."

I faced Kiki. "Speaking of. If you're done with the forensics on the Whitlock case, I hear you've finished up the Gomez testing."

Ross leaned back. "Oh dang. Don't let us hold you up."

Jayda and Ross were aware of the ramifications of the testing. Hirsch had to brief them for the moment we heard the news that the testing was complete. They would be a part of the team when we brought in Paul Xavier. We were all waiting for that moment.

Hirsch said, "It's okay. All of our cases are important."

Blah. Blah. Blah. On with it, my nerves were already in overdrive. "Of course. It's a good update on the Whitlock case. And we should have Xavier in custody soon, and we can ask him about Whitlock. Kiki if you're ready, we're ready."

She nodded. "I have finished all the forensics testing on the Gomez case. As you know, we had previously finished testing clothing found on Este, as well as sequencing the DNA for the sisters and the baby. The remaining evidence collected at Este's grave was analyzed for any substance that would not be native to the area. As well as the testing of the material found under Este and Lori Gomez's fingernails. And finally, I tested the item you provided a few days ago."

Hirsch said, "Thank you for working so quickly."

Was Hirsch as nervous as I was?

Kiki said, "I have a feeling the overtime was worth it."

"Did you find something interesting?" Vincent asked.

"Indeed. First off, the soil collected around Este's grave didn't give us much. All the soil samples contained the expected materials. No foreign particulates that could tie us to a type of grease or paint that might have been introduced from her killer. The fingernail scrapings from Este contained one DNA profile. A match for Paul Xavier. Which we're no longer surprised by. The fingernail clippings from Lori didn't provide any useful information. But we're not too surprised about that either, considering water washes away a lot of evidence." She studied our eager faces and continued. "And last but not least, I was able to get a DNA profile submitted from the coffee mug you provided. The DNA is not in CODIS, so I don't have an identity."

"So, we have nothing?" Vincent asked, eyes wide.

A grin crept up Kiki's face. "Not so fast. The DNA is not in CODIS, but the profile is a match to the DNA profile for the father of Lori's baby."

The group silenced. I didn't know about the rest of them, but I was stunned. I knew he was dirty, but the father of Lori's baby? The secret boyfriend was Sheriff Lafontaine.

Lafontaine had a motive to kill Lori, but we still couldn't figure out why Xavier would kill Este. Was Xavier simply helping his friend? Had Lafontaine killed Lori, and then Xavier killed her sister? Why? Friends who kill together stick together? They couldn't have killed them at the same time. They dumped one in the bay and the other was buried three hours away. What had happened that night? I, for one, was more than eager to arrest Xavier and interview him until he broke.

Kiki said, "I'm guessing you know the identity. Do you need me to leave so that you can discuss?"

I shook my head. "This is highly confidential, but you're already in, right, Hirsch?" I shot a quick look over at Ross and Jayda, who didn't know we'd secretly tested Lafontaine's mug.

Hirsch said, "The mug we submitted for DNA was retrieved from Sheriff Lafontaine's office. It is the coffee mug that he drinks out of every day."

Kiki's large brown eyes widened. "Oh, my."

Ross scrunched up his face. "Y'all are sneaky. How'd you do that?"

Hirsch said, "It's better you don't know."

Jayda said, "Sheriff Lafontaine is the father of Lori Gomez's baby."

"I knew it. So now we arrest them both?" Vincent asked.

He knew it?

"Not exactly," Hirsch said.

"What do you mean?"

"There is no chain of custody for Lafontaine's DNA. So, we know he's the baby's father, but we can't use it until we get his DNA, either willingly or by order."

"Now what?"

Hirsch said, "We need to bring Sarge in on this latest development. I'll go now." With that, Hirsch hurried off.

"Thank you again, Kiki, for doing this so quickly. You can now probably understand the sensitivity and the urgency?"

"I do. Were you surprised by what we found?" she asked, as if she already knew the answer.

"We've had our share of run-ins with Lafontaine, and although I am a little surprised by the results, I'm not as surprised as I should be."

34

MARTINA

"How did you know?"

Vincent said, "I had a feeling."

"You did?" I knew he was guilty for covering it up and knew it was a possibility that Lafontaine was involved in the murder or could be the father, but my gut missed this one.

"Well, when we started talking about how maybe it was Xavier covering for someone else, Lafontaine was the most logical person. Not that I understand killing an innocent person for a friend. But at the time, Lafontaine didn't have any connections in the department like Xavier did. And they're best friends."

Ross said, "I guess it makes sense, if you'd be willing to kill for your best friend."

An unsettling feeling washed over me. "If they killed for each other, they're pretty unlikely to roll over on one another."

"Yep."

I let out a breath. Would Lafontaine walk free? I knew as well as the next investigator that although Lafontaine had motive to kill Lori, we didn't have any physical evidence tying him to her death.

Kiki said, "Well, it sounds like you have your hands full, and I need to get back to the lab. Let me know if you need anything."

"Thanks." Kiki walked out, and I turned to the team. "Big day." Although we had uncovered solid motives, and Xavier's DNA linked him to Este's murder, there were still a lot of unanswered questions about what happened the night of Lori's and Este's murders.

"I'll say," Vincent added.

A few moments later, Sarge and Hirsch burst into the squad room. "It's go time."

WITH ONE PATROL car for backup, Hirsch and I hustled to the entrance of the San Ramon City Hall, ready to take down Paul Xavier. Hirsch turned to me. "You ready?"

"I was ready last week."

With a smirk, Hirsch pulled open the door and rushed up to the reception desk. He pulled out his badge. "My name is Detective Hirsch, with the CoCo County Sheriff's department. I'm here to see Paul Xavier."

"Do you have an appointment?" the woman behind the desk asked.

"No, but we need to see him now."

The woman studied our faces. "Okay. One minute, please." She picked up the receiver and whispered to somebody on the phone and then slowly returned the receiver to its base. She said, "I'm sorry, but he's in a meeting right now. Can I take a message or make an appointment?"

"Where is his office?" Hirsch asked.

"It's down the hall on the left, but you can't go in there without an appointment..."

Hirsch and I didn't hesitate. Hirsch charged down the hallway. Not exactly running, but he was at a good speed.

We reached the office, and Hirsch opened the door.

The mayor, whom I recognized by his sandy brown hair and pale blue eyes, said, "What are you doing? You can't be in here."

"Paul Xavier, can you please stand up?"

"What is this about?"

Hirsch lifted the warrant. "Paul Xavier, I have a warrant for your arrest."

"This is absurd. What is the charge?"

Hirsch handed him the warrant, and the mayor stood up and studied the paper. His face paled.

"Paul Xavier, you are under arrest for the murder of Esther Gomez. Please put your hands behind your back."

The mayor's eyes widened as Hirsch cuffed him and began to read his rights. "You have the right to remain silent..."

"Call the sheriff. I'm sure this is a mistake. We're friends."

I said, "Oh, we know how you're connected to Sheriff Lafontaine. We know everything." It was a lie, but Xavier didn't need to know that.

"This is ridiculous," he spat.

Hirsch paid no mind as he continued to read him his rights. Soon, the mayor's worry turned to rage. "You don't know who you're messing with. I'll have your badge for this. You'll never work in law enforcement ever again."

Staring into the mayor's eyes, I said, "I wouldn't be so sure about that." I had been waiting for this moment since the second Kiki told us his DNA was a match to the profile found on Este's remains. It wasn't lost on me that the mayor's world was about to crumble, as well as everyone associated with him and his crimes.

After Hirsch cuffed him, he pushed him down the hallway. As we reached the reception area, Xavier yelled out, "Patty, call my lawyer and Sheriff Lafontaine."

I wasn't sure who or where this Patty person was, but the entire office was staring at us.

This wasn't the usual protocol for arrests, but because of the discretion needed, we didn't have an entire team with us to arrest Xavier. We hadn't thought he was armed and dangerous considering he was sitting at City Hall.

As we made our way out to the parking lot, everyone in the surrounding area was staring and talking madly amongst themselves.

Hirsch secured the mayor in the back seat carefully and shut the door. I turned around and looked at our passenger. "Are you comfortable back there?"

He glared at me. Jeez. I was simply questioning him about his comfort level. If he wasn't comfortable at that moment, I could only imagine how he would feel after thirty minutes in an interview room. Would he spill his guts or stay silent? Would he implicate Lafontaine? It didn't matter if he did or not, but it would help us out. My gut said Xavier had gotten away with multiple crimes, but he would not get away with this one.

35

HIRSCH

With Paul Xavier simmering quietly in the conference room, I walked over and removed his handcuffs, one by one. He rubbed his wrists after his hands were free. "I want my phone call."

"Of course."

"But before we do that, there are a few things we want to talk to you about."

"You know I know the law, right? I'm a lawyer and the mayor of a town. Are you sure you know what you're doing here?"

If looks could kill, Martina and I would be toast.

Martina said, "We know exactly what we're doing. I believe it's you, Mr. Mayor, who is in over your head."

I glanced at Martina. I liked it when she played tough guy. She was good at it, and I believed it was her true nature. She could be loving and supportive, but she didn't like bad guys, and she wasn't afraid to show it. That or she couldn't contain it. The jury was still out on which it was.

Staring into the mayor's icy blue eyes, I said, "I'm just going to tell it to you as we see it. We've been investigating the missing persons case for a set of sisters, Loretta and Esther Gomez.

They went missing twenty years ago and were never found. That's not all. We realized they were never even input into the missing persons database."

"I don't see how any of this has anything to do with me."

"We'll get to it," Martina added, with snark.

"We found that strange. My team and I were trying to figure out why an officer wouldn't enter two missing persons into the database. Because we're peace officers, we're public servants. We are here to serve our community. And you know what, Mayor Xavier?"

"Don't waste your time, Detective. This whole thing is ludicrous."

It would be a joyful day when the judge handed down this guy's life sentence. "Too late. You made sure that the Gomez sisters' case remained cold, didn't you? And so my team had to waste our time, as you put it, to find the Gomez sisters."

"You're going to regret this."

Martina said, "I don't think so. But I'm betting you are full of regret right about now."

"You see, the thing is, we found Loretta and Esther Gomez. It wasn't even that hard. Because they weren't in the missing persons database, they were never matched up against any Jane Does found in the Bay Area. Our researcher found them within a couple of days. Days, Mr. Xavier." I leaned over and said, "That's right. We found the body of Esther Gomez buried in a shallow grave in Calaveras County. The remains were discovered five years ago and entered into the database with details that matched up with Esther Gomez. She would have been identified five years ago if somebody had input her information into the missing persons database."

The mayor sat silently.

I continued, "In case you forgot, it was your cousin David Xavier who was responsible for investigating that missing persons case. It got me thinking. Why hadn't this missing persons, now homicide, case been solved yet? And you know what I think? I think you instructed your cousin to not investigate, not to put them in the database, and to label them runaways."

Xavier shook his head. "You're going to be so sorry about this. You'll have a hard time getting a job at mall security when I'm done with you."

Not a chance. I would enjoy watching the look on his face when we dropped the bomb that we had his DNA at the crime scene.

"Hold off on calling your buddies, Paul. When everyone finds out what you did, nobody is going to help you. Just wait for it." Martina leaned against the wall with a smug look on her face. She was loving this.

"Thanks, Martina. We also found the remains of Loretta Gomez, and the thing about her is that they found her in the bay. Her remains were recovered twenty years ago and labeled Jane Doe but never matched up because, like I mentioned earlier, she was not input into the missing persons database. What we learned about Loretta or Lori Gomez's body is that she was actually four months pregnant. And the most amazing thing is..." I paused for effect. "The fetus was still intact."

"The miracle of life," Martina added.

Xavier raised his hands in the air. "Get to the point. I have a meeting in an hour. I'm a very busy person."

Xavier was either really confident or great at bluffing. My guess was it was a confidence that was about to be crushed.

Martina smirked. "You'll want to clear your schedule."

"You may recognize us from the news a few years ago. We solved a few hard cases, cases people thought couldn't be solved. But we did. And we solved this one. Are you curious yet?"

Xavier remained steely.

"We found and identified the remains of the Gomez sisters, and thanks to our excellent forensics department, they could retrieve male DNA from Esther's remains. The killer's DNA."

Xavier looked away and didn't meet my eye contact. He knew we had him. "That's right. We recovered your DNA on a shirt and a scarf found on the remains of Esther Gomez. Maybe you didn't remember that you murdered her all those years ago when you made a big show of submitting your DNA on live television, when that little girl went missing in your neighborhood. But, you see, that DNA was put into a database so we could make a positive match. It's over, Xavier."

It was over for Xavier, but there were other fish that needed to be fried.

Xavier turned and stared me dead in the eyes. "I'm not saying a single word without my lawyer. This conversation is over."

After lifting myself out of the chair, I leaned against the wall and placed my arms across my chest. "Remain silent. That's your right. But my partner is going to tell you what else we found. Take it away, Martina."

I knew she was going to love letting him have it. Martina said, "Thanks, Hirsch. That's not the only DNA we found. We also have a DNA profile for Loretta's unborn child. What do you think we found?"

Xavier shifted his gaze to the floor.

"That's right. Your pal, Sheriff Lafontaine, can't help you out here. Because he's in as much hot water as you are. Still nothing to say about that?"

Nodding, I said, "I suppose that's a smart thing to do. What would you do, Martina?"

"Well, first, I wouldn't murder anybody because I'm not a murderer like Mayor Xavier. But if somebody accused me of murder, I would definitely not talk without a lawyer.

Although, if they had found my DNA mixed with the victim's blood, I might look at striking a deal. Trying to save my butt, I'd say who helped me kill Lori and Este and cover it up. I think I'd figure, why not, because there's no way I'd be avoiding jail time. There's just no way. Physical evidence is indisputable. Yeah, I would try to make a deal. That's what I would do."

The two of us stared down at the mayor of San Ramon. He shook his head. "I want my phone call."

"You got it. I'll leave you here for a minute with my partner, Martina. Don't worry, there's a guard outside the door, so you don't need to be too scared of her."

Martina nodded.

I said, "I'll talk to you later," and exited the interview room.

The officer outside the door said, "Is that the mayor who is running for governor?"

"It is. But you need to keep that quiet and make sure he doesn't go anywhere."

"Yes, sir."

Standing next to the interview room, I texted Sarge.

We're back. Xavier's in interview one.

I waited.

Sarge texted back.

We're in my office.

Heart pounding, I hurried over to Sarge's office to confront my superior's superior. Though I was confident we were doing the right thing, what Xavier said wasn't entirely wrong. If, for some reason, this went sideways, despite the physical evidence, I would be out of a job and would never work in law enforcement again. My credibility would be ruined and the Cold Case Squad disbanded. No pressure.

I knocked on the door and from his seat, the sheriff opened it. I walked in and shut the door behind me, then leaned up against the door. "Sarge. Sheriff."

"Would you like to give the sheriff an update on your recent arrest?"

Yes, and no. "Sheriff, we have arrested the prime suspect in the murder of Esther Gomez."

The sheriff's bright blue eyes widened.

"Este Gomez went missing twenty years ago, and her remains were found five years ago, but no identification was made and they labeled her a Jane Doe. That was because the department didn't input her into the missing persons database, and we think that's because the person responsible for that activity was David Xavier, the officer who took the missing persons report and also the cousin of Paul Xavier, our prime suspect."

I watched the sheriff's reaction. His face didn't give many tells, but he lost two shades of pigment and was nearing sheet white. Part of me didn't believe Lafontaine had anything to do with the murders and had been aghast to learn that he was the father of Lori's baby. But standing there, I could see he was guilty. Without a doubt.

"We have forensic evidence, specifically DNA, from Esther's body, on a scarf and mixed with her blood from her neck and chest. She had been stabbed sixteen times."

The sheriff flinched. But silence remained in Sarge's office. I needed to make it very clear to the sheriff that we understood his involvement. "From our research, we understand that you, Sheriff Lafontaine, and Paul Xavier have been friends since childhood. In order to ensure that Xavier paid for what he did, we had to keep the investigation quiet."

"I could have your badge for this," the sheriff threatened, albeit half-heartedly.

"We know you were dating Esther Gomez's sister, Lori. And we know you were the father of Lori's baby."

The sheriff shook his head. "This is ridiculous. You have absolutely no proof."

I glanced over at Sarge and back at the sheriff. I'd had run-ins with supervisors before. It was how I had landed at the CoCo County Sheriff's Department in the first place. But it was one thing to disagree with how someone handled a case and quite another to stare down the sheriff and tell him you are going to send him to prison. "We have evidence that you are the father of Lori's baby."

"That's impossible."

"It's not. We got a hold of your DNA. You are the child's father."

The sheriff looked away. He knew we had him. How would he justify what he had done?

Lafontaine turned back to stare into my eyes. "Even if I was the child's father, it doesn't prove that I killed her."

"Are you saying you are the father of Lori's baby?"

The sheriff nodded. "I knew she was pregnant. I didn't know what she did with the baby."

"So, you are the father of Lori's child?" Sarge asked.

I understood the need to ask him to repeat the answer. The admission was shocking.

"Yes, I was the father, but it doesn't mean I killed her."

After a knowing glance at Sarge and back to the sheriff, I said, "How do you know that Lori was killed?"

I gave him an *I got you* smile. "Because you killed her, and you had your friend Paul Xavier help kill her sister. You're a disgrace to the badge, *sir*."

Despite the sweat trickling down the side of the sheriff's face, he said, "You can't prove any of this."

"Oh, but we can and have. Xavier is in interview one. We have his DNA at the scene, and we have your DNA and your admission that you are the father of Lori's baby."

"Maybe what you're saying is true, and Paul killed Este, but I don't see how any of that has anything to do with me. There is no evidence I hurt those girls."

"Not yet. Consider this a courtesy call."

The sheriff turned to Sarge. "You knew about this?"

"Hirsch has kept me up to speed throughout the investigation," Sarge said. "I see this happening one of two ways. You give us your DNA willingly and admit your role in the Gomez sisters' murders or we get a warrant for your DNA and a search warrant for your house and any property you may own that could have evidence linking you to the murders. A connection to Xavier alone would give us enough probable cause."

I added, "And you could resign immediately."

Lafontaine stood up and growled, "Get your warrants." He pushed me back, flung the door open, and stormed off.

"That went well."

Sarge shook his head. "Write up the warrants for Lafontaine, and I'll get some resources to keep an eye on him. We don't need him going and destroying any evidence."

"I'll get right on it. Thanks." I didn't envy Sarge. We were about to take down two of our own. But were they ever really one of ours? They weren't public servants — they only served themselves.

36

LORI

Snuggling next to Freddie, I felt like everything was right. All my fears about the baby and his earlier rejection had melted away. The day after I told him about the pregnancy, we met up, and it was like a switch had been flipped. He apologized with tears in his eyes. He said, "I'm sorry for not fighting for you before. I should have stood up to my family. I should have picked you." I had tried to interrupt and tell him I forgave him, but he stopped me. "There's more. I told my parents about the baby and that I want to be with you. They said they want to meet you."

It was like all my dreams had come true, and I was proud of myself for not giving up on us. We embraced and made love. It was magical.

Since that night, he had treated me like a queen. He sent me flowers at my work and called to say he was thinking about me. He even bought me a gold necklace with two hearts intertwined that I hadn't taken off since the moment he gave it to me.

Admittedly, I had a few doubts with the sudden turnaround in his treatment of me and that it had been three weeks and I still hadn't met his parents, but I had to believe he was sincere. Este's opinion of Freddie had not changed. She said she trusted him even less than she had before. She thought he was only being sweet to ensure I got rid of the baby.

Freddie may have been afraid of his parents, which wasn't my favorite thing about him, but he wouldn't pretend to love me just so I didn't go through with the pregnancy. That was far-fetched. I ignored her crazy fears and chalked it up to her caring about me and wanting the best for me. Yes, Freddie and I had a rocky period, but I moved past it and continued with my eyes set on our future.

Despite the daily morning sickness and the exhaustion of growing a human inside of me, I was happy. Content. And I could go to school and work and see Freddie without too much extra effort. Although having changed my bedtime from midnight to ten o'clock, I was having a difficult time staying awake during our drive-in movie dates. Freddie loved to watch movies at the drive-in theater. He said it was because it gave us privacy, unlike at a movie theater or out at a restaurant. He turned to me and traced the side of my face with his fingertip. "You're so beautiful."

"Stop it."

Not that I meant it. I loved it when he complimented me.

"Stop being so beautiful."

I turned up and kissed him. He said, "I'm so thankful you took me back, after how I treated you. I promise it'll never happen again."

My heart glowed.

He sat up, and I did the same. "I've been thinking about us and our future."

"You have?" I didn't know he thought about those things. He hadn't brought it up before. But if he asked me if I thought about our future, I would have whipped out a diagram of our next fifty years. We would get married and then the baby would come, and we would live in a small apartment together. When we were done with school and had enough money, we would buy a small house with a fence in the front yard and a backyard swing set for the baby. And as Freddie grew in his career and I grew in mine, we would upgrade to a bigger house and have more children. At least two more. I had always wanted a big, happy family. And on the weekends, Este would visit with her family and children. We would drink Arnold Palmers while we watched the cousins play in the yard. I thought life was going to be so good.

"I have. I love you and you love me, so I was thinking. I plan to go to UC Berkeley and will graduate in two years. You can go there too, or to another Bay Area university. For after your undergrad, we can start mapping out medical schools in California to make sure that we stay close to each other."

"That sounds great."

Not exactly what I had expected. Obviously, we would need to be close together, and it was sweet that he was thinking about the logistics. But what about marriage? We were having a baby. And I wanted to be married. Not that I had told him that. "There are plenty of colleges and medical schools in California."

"Exactly. So, I was thinking, after college maybe we can get an apartment together."

After college? The baby would arrive well before then. "That sounds great, Freddie."

Why did I say that? It didn't sound great. It was missing one major component. Our baby.

"I feel so lucky to have found you. And that I don't have to go through life searching for my other half because I already found you."

That sounded like forever. I wanted forever. "I agree, and I love you so much."

"And I've been thinking about your pregnancy."

Finally. The baby elephant in the room. "And?"

"I want to have a baby with you, but not yet. I don't think this is the baby that was meant for us. It would be too hard. I'm still in school, you're in school, and we both live at home. We're still kids ourselves."

He wanted me but not the baby? "What are you saying?"

"I think you should get an abortion. I'll pay for it. You don't have to worry about a thing."

I gasped. Not worry about a thing? "You want me to get rid of the baby?"

"If this was five years from now, I would never even recommend that. I want a life with you. I just don't think this is the right time for a baby. We have plenty of time to make another baby. We certainly had fun making this one, right?"

I didn't know what to make of this. Having a baby terrified me, but this one was already here. The future was no guarantee, and the more I thought about getting rid of it, the more I wasn't sure I could actually do it. It was my body and my choice, but I didn't think I could choose that. Freddie, my love, and I made it. A family with Freddie was what I wanted. "I don't know, Freddie." I shook my head and squeezed my eyes shut, wishing this would just go away. This conversation and this idea. I didn't want to break down crying, but I did because I was angry and sad and frustrated and confused.

He pulled me closer. "Shh. It's okay, babe. Don't cry. We don't have to get rid of the baby. I was thinking it might be a good idea, but this is your choice. If you want to keep it, we do it together."

My tears stopped, and I looked him in the eyes. "You mean it?"

"I mean it."

After a sweet kiss, I snuggled back up with him and continued watching the movie. I had everything I wanted, Freddie and our baby, yet an uneasiness remained inside me.

37

MARTINA

With Paul Xavier at booking, Hirsch and I stood outside the conference room, discussing what had happened in Sarge's office. Hirsch was clearly shaken from the interaction and Lafontaine's admission that he was the father of Lori's baby. "Do you want to take a break before we interview David Xavier? Jayda and Ross won't let him out of their sight."

It had been a long day, and it wasn't over yet. Would David confess to helping cover up his cousin's crime?

"No, I'm fine. But boy, will I be happy when this case is closed and everyone who needs to be behind bars is behind bars."

From his explanation, it sounded like Lafontaine would not go down without a fight. "Okay, let's do it."

Hirsch knocked on the door. It opened, and Jayda appeared. "You ready?"

"Yeah."

She stepped outside. "Everything okay?"

Hirsch raked his fingers through his hair. "Do I look that bad?"

Hirsch's expression was grim, but before Jayda could say anything about it, I explained what had happened. "Oh, dang."

"Has David said anything?" Hirsch asked, clearly not wanting to discuss Lafontaine further.

"We explained what we have on Paul, but David wouldn't talk. His lawyer is on the way. I think he'll be a tough nut to crack."

"Thanks, Jayda. We'll let you know when we're done questioning him about the Gomez sisters, and you can nail him on Whitlock."

"Cool."

"Let's go, Hirsch." I pushed open the door.

Ross stood near the man, who sat smugly with his hands on the table. Ross gave us a head nod and exited. After introductions, I sat across from David Xavier, someone who made a pledge to serve others and to find the missing but had been an accomplice to his cousin, Paul Xavier and Sheriff Lafontaine's murderous activities. In my mind, he was almost just as guilty. Hirsch said, "Thank you for waiting. We appreciate it."

David Xavier had the same icy blue eyes as his cousin. He said, "Not a problem. I've got nothing to hide. I was on the force a long time, and between you and me, I am shocked by these allegations against Paul. There must be a mistake."

I was pretty sure David Xavier knew there was no mistake. He was just trying to figure out how he hadn't covered their tracks well enough. "I assure you there is no mistake. Your cousin Paul murdered Esther Gomez. And we're pretty sure you helped him cover it up."

"I did nothing of the sort."

Hirsch said, "Do you remember taking the missing persons report from Araceli Cruz, Esther and Loretta Gomez's aunt?"

"I do because it was unusual. Twins. But they were adults.

Two college kids — they could have gone anywhere. They likely were just out on a long weekend."

"But they weren't. They were dead. Your cousin killed at least one of them."

David raised his hands in defense. "I have no knowledge of that whatsoever."

Hirsch said, "And you didn't think to investigate what happened to Lori and Este? We have the file and there's hardly anything in it. Not only that, but the two young women weren't even input into the missing persons database. That was your job."

"Twenty years ago, I was new to missing persons and homicide. If they weren't entered into the missing persons database, I must have forgotten. If they weren't in there, I apologize. It was an innocent mistake."

Innocent? Right.

A knock sounded. Hirsch stood up and poked his head out. He returned with a man in a suit, who handed Hirsch a business card. "My name is Blane Zuckerman, and I'm Mr. Xavier's lawyer."

After a few handshakes, I offered, "Have a seat."

Mr. Zuckerman sat next to his client.

The lawyer said, "I spoke briefly with my client. I'd like to hear the charges against him, and if there aren't any, we're done here."

Hirsch sat down across from the lawyer. "No charges have been filed yet. But we believe your client was an accessory after the fact in the murder of Esther Gomez."

"Do you have reason to believe, or do you have evidence?" the lawyer asked.

David Xavier gave a smug smile.

"We have his cousin, Paul Xavier, being booked on murder charges for killing Esther Gomez as we speak. Your client took the missing persons report for Esther Gomez and her sister Loretta. He didn't investigate the missing persons or add their details to the missing persons database."

David said, "As I explained earlier, it was an innocent mistake. I was new to the department back then. I must have missed it. And I apologize for that."

The lawyer nodded. "That sounds reasonable. It's obvious there was no malice towards these girls. He didn't omit them from the missing person database on purpose. I'm afraid you don't have a case."

Shaking my head at their arrogance, I said, "We could've brought closure to their family years ago when the girls' remains were found if they had been in the missing persons database. Because of your mistake, their family did not know what happened to them for twenty years. Do you have any idea what that's like?"

David shook his head. "I don't, but I can imagine it's awful. Like I said, my deepest apology to the family."

Hirsch said, "We'll be sure to relay the message."

Good, Hirsch wasn't going to be nice to the guy just because he used to be on the force. But then again, one of Hirsch's biggest pet peeves was a dirty cop, and I think we were both convinced that David Xavier was a dirty cop.

The lawyer stood up. "It sounds like we're done here."

"Before you go, my detectives have a few other questions for David."

The lawyer sat down.

Hirsch left the room and returned with Jayda and Ross. I gave up my seat for Jayda and Ross to go in for the kill.

Jayda thanked me for the seat and said, "Hi again. My partner, Ross, and I are working a case. A man named Richard Whitlock was murdered ten years ago. He was stabbed to death, around midnight, at a park in San Ramon. Do you know who the responding officer to that scene was?"

David's face lost its jovial expression. He didn't know we knew about Richard Whitlock. Jayda set a file on the table and flipped it open. "It's the funniest thing. When my partner and I picked up the cold case, we had our team check all the electronic files for it. The responding officer was listed as Jeff Grayson, but do you know what we found in Grayson's notes?"

David said, "I don't remember the case."

Lie.

"There was a note that said you were at the scene when Grayson arrived. It took us a beat to figure that out because he referred to you as DX. Did you know you were the only officer with the initials DX at the time?"

The lawyer said, "If you have a point, get to it. Otherwise, we're leaving."

Jayda tapped the file. "Well, that's not all we found. We found Whitlock worked for your cousin, Paul Xavier."

"Is there a question?" the lawyer asked.

"Why were you at the scene of Richard Whitlock's murder?"

David Xavier whispered to his lawyer. The lawyer nodded and said, "If there's no other questions about the Gomez case, we're done here."

I said, "Before you go, a little food for thought. These are two random files we picked up. What else will we find if we search for cases with the Xavier name associated with it? I bet the press would have a field day with what we find."

David swallowed. The lawyer said. "We're done here."

Hirsch added, "Pass along the note to your cousin. Every single thing we find on you and Paul during our investigations will make headlines. We will make sure every single detail is exposed. Your family will be ruined. As of now, we've held the

details pretty close to the chest. But if we don't get any cooperation from you or Paul, we'll have no choice but to make your
family's indiscretions public. We can give you a day or two to
think about it."

David Xavier stood up. "Have a good day, detectives. Ms.
Monroe." And he walked out with his lawyer trailing behind.

To the room, I said, "Well, he gave us nothing other than a
guilty look."

Jayda said, "He absolutely knows more than he is telling us.
He covered up both cases. And I wouldn't be surprised if David
had a hand in Whitlock's murder. You saw how he shut down
fast when we told him Grayson listed him in the notes."

I said, "I did. We need to get them talking. Xavier or
Lafontaine. Can Greggs make a deal to get one of them to talk?"
I didn't care who. They were all guilty.

Hirsch said, "I'll call Greggs after I put in the warrant
requests for Lafontaine."

Jayda said, "You need some help, Hirsch? We could draft
the warrant requests."

"I'd appreciate it."

We gathered our things and exited the interview room. All I
could think was, what a day.

38

MARTINA

Hirsch looked worse for the wear. I handed him a steaming cup of sugar and caffeine. "One caramel latte."

"Thanks." He took a sip and sighed. "Just what I needed."

"Good?"

"Yeah."

"You ready to search Lafontaine's house?" It wasn't a question regarding his tactical status. Hirsch had confided in me he had been down about Lafontaine's newfound status of dirty cop. Hirsch was the rock in our partnership most of the time. But this wasn't one of those times. In the past two years, we had uncovered multiple dirty cops, and I thought Hirsch was beginning to question where all the good ones had gone. I tried to remind him they existed, a bunch of them. And he was their leader.

For the first time in a while, I drove us to the scene as multiple squad cars followed behind. We discussed strategy on the way and agreed we didn't expect to find much other than a computer that may have a trail of a cover-up or involvement in the Gomez murders. As I approached the address for Lafontaine's home, in the suburban parts of the East Bay, with pretty lawns and well-maintained, million-dollar homes, it was easy to spot. It was the one with news vans and reporters with camera crews standing outside. It hadn't taken long for the press to catch wind of what was happening.

Parked, Hirsch instructed the team, and we headed to the front door. He knocked three times, and the door opened. Sheriff Lafontaine was not happy to see us. Between the warrant and his paid leave pending our investigation, we were officially his least favorite people. "Sir, we have a warrant to search your property." Hirsch handed Lafontaine the paperwork.

The sheriff took it but didn't read it. "C'mon in. The wife and kids are at her parents. Do what you must." He stepped to the side.

Hirsch said, "Much appreciated, sir."

As I sailed past, I smiled like it was my birthday.

The man hated us, but he knew better than to fight it. That or he knew we wouldn't find anything.

THE TEAM SEARCHED Sheriff Lafontaine's house for three hours and came up completely empty-handed, and it wasn't looking good. We had Lafontaine's DNA, which gave us motive but not proof he was responsible for or had been involved in Lori and Este's murder. We needed to find something tying Lafontaine to Lori or Este from the night he and Xavier killed them.

We needed Paul Xavier to talk, but so far, Paul wasn't saying a single word about the case, and to make matters worse, he had made bail. Between Xavier being out on bail and Lafontaine out on administrative leave, all eyes, especially the media's, were on the Cold Case Squad.

The team had been working tirelessly to gather any and all

evidence that could tie them to the murders. And anything to tie Xavier to the death of Richard Whitlock.

No luck.

But Jayda and Ross were continuing to investigate the Whitlock angle and had been questioning the two suspects in the Gerald Ackerman abduction. It was all hands on deck to solve these cases.

The press was saying all kinds of things. Some positive, like the police were finally looking into their own and would clean up City Hall. And some negative like the Cold Case Squad was on a witch hunt. It went without saying Hirsch and I were keeping a pretty low profile and avoiding the press like it was our job.

Defeated, I was walking out the front door when Hirsch came running up with bright eyes. Did he find something?

"They found out Lafontaine has a storage unit just five minutes down the road. We have a warrant. You interested in finding out what he's been storing?"

After I took a second to thank the Lord, I said, "Let's go."

We jogged to my car and hopped in quickly before the press could spot us. "How's it going in there?" Hirsch asked.

"Not good. They packed up a few computers, but that's it."

"My guess is if there's any evidence, it's in that storage unit."

Let's hope so. "Have you heard from Jayda or Ross about the Ackerman case?"

"They've just left Trent Blackwell's and are requesting a warrant to search his house. Jayda said there were some inconsistencies in his answers. They think he's the guy."

"Fingers crossed."

We arrived at the storage facility and looked for the unit number. We parked in front of #13 and hopped out of the car. There weren't any other people around. That was for the best.

We strutted up to the roll-up door and studied the padlock

that secured it from thieves. "I'll run over to the office and see if they have bolt cutters or a key." Hirsch jogged off while I waited for backup. We needed cameras recording before we opened the storage unit. Everything had to be done by the book. We had zero room for accusations of evidence planting. Everything we did had to be documented on video so that there would be no question that what we did was completely legal.

Standing in the spot, I inhaled the warm air and appreciated the sun shining down with just a small smattering of clouds. It was a beautiful day in the Bay Area. It would be even prettier if we could get justice for Lori and Este. It wouldn't be right if only Paul Xavier went down for their murders. I knew Lafontaine was guilty.

Hirsch returned with a man wearing blue jeans and a light blue T-shirt, carrying bolt cutters.

Two patrol cars pulled up, and I waved overhead. Two uniformed officers we knew well approached.

"Camera crew is here."

"Thanks, Olsen. Let's get rolling." Hirsch turned to the man in the blue T-shirt. "All right, we need to film everything. Are you okay to be on film?"

"No problem."

Hirsch nodded, and the man walked over to the padlock and cut it open. Hardly secure. Any old fool with a bolt cutter could get into every storage unit on the lot.

Hirsch and I slipped on some rubber gloves, and I pushed open the rolling door to look inside.

Hirsch called out, "Flashlight, please."

An officer shined a flashlight, and Hirsch pulled the string above to turn on the light in the storage unit.

It was the most organized storage unit I had seen. It contained several rows of stacked boxes and an old dresser, an old mattress, a bed frame, a floor lamp, and what looked like a dining table with more boxes stacked on top. I said, "Let's start with the dresser first. It's the most accessible."

Hirsch said, "Works for me," and we planted ourselves in front of the oak dresser and directed the camera and flashlight for a better view.

Hirsch carefully opened the top drawer. The interior was filled with books, mostly science fiction and fantasy novels, with a few self-help books. We took out each one and flipped through every page. It took considerably longer than we would expect, and we found nothing of use.

We moved down to the next drawer. More books. Was Lafontaine a big reader? Maybe they belonged to his wife? Who was Frederick Lafontaine?

We continued the process but were quickly losing hope we would finish before the weekend. This was just a few drawers and there were dozens of boxes to search. Once the team at the house was done, we would need them to come out to the storage unit.

The bottom drawer of the dresser was filled with comic books and a blanket. I pulled out the comic book, actually a Mad magazine — interesting. I thumbed through it and found nothing unusual other than the whacky content. There was a stack of six more Mad magazines. Was Lafontaine a Mad magazine fan? Did that mean he had a sense of humor? If he did, I hadn't seen it.

I set them on the ground next to the dresser and picked up what looked like a red knit blanket.

Not a blanket.

"Olsen, did you get this?"

He stepped closer. "Yes."

I directed him to zoom in. I lifted it out of the drawer and glanced over at my partner. His eyes widened. "Is that what I think it is?"

We got him.

Staring up at the camera, I said, "For the record, this is a red scarf found at the bottom drawer in the storage unit #13 rented to Frederick Lafontaine."

Carefully, I unfolded the scarf and brought it closer to my face, carefully not touching, and inhaled. There was still a lingering trace of perfume.

Perfume scent meant there were compounds on the scarf. If there was perfume, perhaps there would be perspiration or blood. It could have DNA.

Heart racing, I said, "I need an evidence bag."

One officer ran over and opened up the evidence bag. I slipped the scarf inside and sealed the bag closed. I turned to Hirsch. "We need to get this to the lab immediately. Why don't we call in extra help to get through the rest of the unit?"

Hirsch said, "You and I are the only ones who would know that the scarf is significant."

We had seen the pictures of the two girls wearing the scarves on their last day. Nobody else had. What else was Lafontaine keeping? Would only Hirsch and I be able to determine what may be relevant to the investigation?

"That's a good point." How could we handle this? There may be more evidence to be collected, but the scarf needed to get to the lab. "Let's run it back, and we'll see if anyone from the Cold Case Squad can go through the Gomez photos and help out."

"All right."

Walking out of the storage unit, I stared up at the sky and said a small prayer before handing the evidence bag to Hirsch. Behind the wheel, I said, "We're going to nail him."

"Fingers crossed."

39

MARTINA

Having to wait for the lab results on the scarf was maddening. The fact we were knee deep in paperwork from the searches of Lafontaine and Xavier's properties didn't make it any better. I knew Kiki and the team were working around the clock to test it, but it didn't make the wait any easier. It was the last piece of evidence to test in the sisters' murders. And if the evidence didn't point to the sheriff, it wasn't likely we could arrest Lafontaine unless he confessed or Xavier rolled on him.

Jayda and Ross entered the squad room. "Hey, Hirsch, Martina. We found something."

"What is it?" Progress, please. The Whitlock murder had stalled, with no evidence of murder for hire, no witnesses, and no forensic evidence relating to the killer. There were only the suspicious facts that Whitlock worked for Xavier and David Xavier inexplicably was at the scene when the first responder arrived. As damning as it seemed, David Xavier could easily say he heard it on the radio or use another excuse. Placing him at the scene didn't prove murder. Because of that, Jayda and Ross were fully supporting us and the Ackerman case.

"They completed the dig under the crawl space at Trent

Blackwell's house. They uncovered a skeleton. Dr. Scribner was on the scene and said it looked like it could be the bones of a small child, a boy of about ten to twelve years old. We think we found Gerald Ackerman."

My chest tightened. It was the most likely scenario, but that didn't make it feel good. My heart broke for the Ackermans who may soon learn their son had been dead and buried two blocks from their house.

"Where's the suspect?" Hirsch asked.

"He's in booking. We arrested him on the spot."

Hirsch said, "Excellent work."

A sad win, but a win nonetheless. "When will we be able to confirm if it's Gerald?"

"Dr. Scribner has to perform the autopsy, get dental records, and send samples to the forensics lab. We haven't notified the family yet. You two were the investigators before we took over and have spoken to the parents. Did you want to tell them and get records? If you're too busy, we can handle it."

Before Hirsch could answer, Kiki walked in with a knowing look and a file folder. There was no reason to be covert or use our special conference room. The room silenced. "Hey."

Kiki grinned. "It's done."

"I should get Sarge. Can you wait a minute?"

"Of course."

Hirsch hurried out.

"I have a feeling we're going to owe you a nice lunch after this."

"Lunch? What's that?" she teased.

My stomach was nervous, the anticipation eating at me. Hirsch rushed in, with Sarge by his side.

Kiki said, "Are you ready for this?"

Sarge scratched his head. "As ready as I'm going to be."

Kiki nodded. "We confirmed that Frederick Lafontaine is

the father of Loretta Gomez's baby. Not a surprise, from what I understand. Besides testing the swab, we took several pieces from the red scarf and analyzed for DNA and other particulates. The scarf had DNA from two contributors, one Loretta Gomez. The second is a match for Frederick Lafontaine."

"Lafontaine kept Lori's scarf as a souvenir?" Jayda asked.

"It appears so."

"Why?" That was the question. Was it a creepy souvenir like serial killers liked to keep? Or a memento? Or did he keep it because there was evidence of their involvement?

Hirsch said, "Who knows?"

"Well, we have the photo of the two sisters wearing the scarves the night they disappeared. Presumably, the night they were killed. Which means he was with Lori that night. He was at a minimum one of the last people to see her alive."

Sarge said, "But it doesn't prove he killed her."

"No, but the fact he had it will be difficult to explain without looking guilty."

"Do we have enough for an arrest warrant?" I asked.

All eyes were on Sarge. "Lafontaine is the father of Lori's baby, and he was in possession of the scarf that she was wearing the last time she was seen alive. It may be enough for a warrant. Let me talk to the DA. I don't want to arrest him if we can't prosecute him."

Hirsch said, "Maybe he'd be willing to talk to us voluntarily?"

"To what? Give him a chance to explain. Do you really think he'll talk?" I asked.

"Maybe. There is no direct evidence that he killed her. The only physical evidence we have is the blood from Xavier on Este."

"It's weak, but could they put together the story? I see it as Lafontaine had to get rid of Lori because she was pregnant. He was with her the night she died — the scarf proves it. He brings his buddy Paul to help. Este witnesses the whole thing and Paul kills her. They drive her out to Calaveras County bury her and the secret lasts for twenty years."

I glanced back up at Kiki. "Is there any other testing that could be done?"

"I'm afraid not. We've exhausted all the test articles, but we can take a second look."

Hirsch said, "Everything is circumstantial. It's damning, but it's circumstantial. Sarge, do you think you could get him down here to talk to us?"

"I'll call him. Between us, I don't think the DA will prosecute with what we have unless we can get Paul Xavier to turn on him. And he's still not talking."

"Do we have anything that could get him to talk?" I asked.

Hirsch said, "DA Greggs is working on it. He's thinking if we take the death penalty off the table, Xavier might talk. He's working on a backup offer. Reduced sentence and charges. Not great, but it might be what it takes to get him and Lafontaine."

That was how it went more often than not. Awful murderers only serving twenty-years in order to implicate their accomplice. If only there was another way, but I couldn't see it.

Hirsch said, "Okay, Sarge's calling Lafontaine. And Jayda and Ross, we need to go to the Ackermans." He turned to Kiki. "Thank you, Kiki. You and your team have been instrumental in this case."

"You're very welcome."

I added, "We'll do lunch next week. Our treat."

Certain more than ever that Lafontaine had a hand in Lori's death, and likely Este's, it was frustrating that we didn't have any physical evidence proving he had participated in the murder. Who knows, maybe Lafontaine would fess up. Stranger things had happened. Sarge and Kiki said their goodbyes and exited, nearly at the same time as Vincent plodded in. "What did I miss?"

We explained, and he said, "Guess we'll be looking for a new sheriff."

He wasn't wrong. Even if we couldn't charge Lafontaine, there was no way he'd survive the rest of his term, let alone a reelection campaign. As soon as the press learned of the details of the circumstantial evidence and his connection to Lori and Xavier, they would eat him alive.

40

LORI

With the phone up to my ear, I suppressed screaming with joy. "Okay, sure. Yeah, that sounds great."

"And you remember the spot?" Freddie asked.

"I do."

"Okay, I'll see you then. I love you."

My heart warmed. "I love you too." I hung up the phone and squealed, "Oh my gosh, you're never going to believe this."

Este sat cross-legged on her twin bed, directly across from me. "What?"

"That was Freddie. He says he wants to meet on the bridge at ten pm tomorrow night."

Este scrunched up her face. "Why?"

Grinning like an idiot, I said, "He said he has a big question to ask me."

"Why at ten o'clock at night on a bridge?" Este asked with a suspicious tone.

She just didn't get it. "It's the bridge we walked across on our first date and had our first kiss. I think he's going to propose!" I squealed.

Este frowned. "You think he's going to propose?"

"What else would he have to ask me?"

"I don't know, but you've never discussed marriage, have you?"

Ever since I told Freddie about the baby, our relationship was like a fairytale. Well, it was once he stopped asking me to get rid of the baby. I forgave him for that. It was a lot to process. Neither of us envisioned we would start a family at that point in our lives. I thought he just needed more time. It was an enormous step to start a family. And that was what we were doing. It was like we were back at the beginning of our relationship. He was attentive. He was sweet. Every day, he told me I glowed and was more beautiful than the next, and that he was so happy we had found each other. "No, we haven't talked about marriage, but we have discussed what it would be like to have a baby."

"A proposal is kind of a stretch from that. Maybe he wants to see if you want to get an apartment together?"

Could that be the question? That wasn't nearly as exciting. "I still think it's a proposal. His family is kind of old fashioned. They'll probably want us to be engaged before we're living together."

The middle of the Alameda bridge was the most romantic moment in our history except for that night at the cabin when we sat outside, staring at the moon while holding one another. It had to be a proposal. That's it. Moonlight. First kiss.

"I don't know. I don't want you to get your hopes up and be disappointed."

I shook my head. "No, I think it's a proposal. It has to be a proposal. It totally fits."

"I don't know," Este said.

"Well, I'm sure. You never trusted him. But look how he's been treating me. Other than that little blip, he's wonderful."

"You seem happy, but he still doesn't pick you up at the house, and you've still met none of his friends or family."

My gut stirred. It was true. I had been disappointed the meeting hadn't taken place, and I worried Freddie's parents still weren't sure about me. Maybe they needed a little more time after all. "I think he's giving them more time to get used to the idea. His family has never dated or married outside their race and..."

"What?" Este's eyes actually bulged out of her head. I hadn't told her the reason Freddie had broken up with me was because his parents didn't approve of him dating a brown girl because I knew she would flip out. Understandably. If I didn't love Freddie so deeply, I would have walked away as soon as I learned they didn't approve of me because of my race. It certainly didn't make Freddie's parents sound like good people. I stared at my naked left hand and said, "It's fine. He says at first they were a little concerned, but now that we're having a baby, they have accepted him dating a Latina."

Este looked horrified. "Do you hear yourself?"

"Look. Freddie wants to be with me. He talked to them and let them know he was serious about me and now they're okay with it." I stared down at my naked hand again, imagining a big diamond ring — an heirloom from the family. I would be Mrs. Loretta Lafontaine. It had a ring to it.

"Maybe, but..."

Este wasn't convinced, but she would be after Freddie and I were engaged. I clasped my hands together. "Please be happy for me."

"You're probably right. I am happy for you."

With that, I jumped off the bed and screamed and wrapped my arms around Este. "Can you believe it? Tomorrow night will be the biggest night of my life."

She squeezed me back and said, "Congratulations."

I released her. "You'll be there, right?" I wanted to document the entire night.

"Are you sure?"

"Well, we're driving separately, but after he gets down on one knee on the bridge and says, 'Loretta Gomez, I love you and want you to be my wife, will you marry me,' we'll want to celebrate together. You can take the car back after we hug and take pictures."

We screamed with excitement.

A knock on our bedroom door grabbed my attention. "Come in."

Auntie walked in. "What is all the screaming about?"

"It's a surprise. But I'll be able to tell you after tomorrow night!"

Auntie looked confused. "Okay, then I look forward to tomorrow night."

I still hadn't had the guts to tell Auntie about Freddie because I knew she would expect him to come to dinner and to pick me up at the door. She was old fashioned like that. I figured we would wait until after I met his family and we were engaged.

"Me too."

Soon, everything would be just the way it was meant to be. I thought this was the end of the world as I knew it, the start of a whole new plan, a whole new life, and that it would be hard and scary, but now I realized it was exactly the path that I was meant to be on. I knew the first day I met Freddie he would change my life. There was so much to look forward to. The future was so close, and I couldn't wait.

41

HIRSCH

Outside the conference room, Martina, Sarge, and I listened as District Attorney Greggs explained the situation. "Lafontaine's here with his lawyer. He's agreed to come down and talk to us, but that's it. From what Hirsch has explained, we don't have enough to prosecute him. He will have to confess if you want to arrest him. If you can't get him to confess, you'll need to get Xavier to implicate Lafontaine. If not, Lafontaine will walk on this one."

"On murder?" Martina asked with wide eyes and hands on her hips.

"We don't have any physical evidence proving that he killed her."

"But we have the scarf with her and his DNA on it. There's a photo of her and her sister wearing that exact scarf the night they were killed."

"But they were dating, so finding his DNA isn't strange."

Martina countered, "But the fact he had it in his possession is."

"That's true. It may be compelling to a jury, but he's a sitting sheriff. It'll be tough to prove beyond a reasonable doubt. Best case, we need bulletproof physical evidence. Or if Paul Xavier corroborates Lafontaine was at the scene of the crime, and he helped kill one or both of the sisters."

"Are you offering Xavier a deal?"

Greggs nodded. "I sent the first one to his lawyer. It was rejected. We're working on a second."

Martina said, "We need to turn up the heat. Get one or both of them to talk."

Greggs said, "I'll let you get to it."

"Thanks."

The group waved as he left.

"How do we play this? Martina and I know the case inside and out. We should question him. Assuming Martina can be nice."

She gave a big old fake smile. "Nice is my middle name."

Sarge said, "Actually, I wonder if Martina should stay out here."

Martina's smile disappeared. "Why?"

Sarge glanced at Martina. "He's not exactly your biggest fan."

"Yes, he hates me. But maybe he hates me enough that he loses his cool and tells us what happened."

She had a point.

Sarge conceded. "Well then, do us proud."

Sarge was a smart man, and he was dating Martina's mother. He knew it was best not to make comments on her personality. Martina was a lovely woman. Caring, empathetic, tough, emotionally and physically, but she didn't like it when people weren't straight with her, and she had a really hard time hiding it. If she even tried. She was one of those people whose facial expressions gave her away every time. "Let's do it."

The sheriff and his lawyer were already seated. Lafontaine looked confident. Our job was to change that. We stood in front of them, and I extended my hand to the lawyer. "I'm Detective Hirsch."

"Roger Caddel. I'm representing Frederick Lafontaine."

Martina said, "Martina Monroe. I'm Hirsch's partner."

They shook hands, and we took a seat. Mr. Caddel said, "I'm assuming you don't need introductions."

"No, we are familiar."

Mr. Caddel said, "Great. So, this is how it is going to go. You tell us what you have, and we'll answer any questions that we feel are appropriate."

This would either be the pinnacle of my career or the downfall. We needed to prove Lafontaine was guilty. I had to go with my instincts and Martina's gut on this one. Lafontaine was guilty. He knew it and we knew it. We just had to prove it so Greggs could prosecute him.

"Loretta and Esther Gomez went missing twenty years ago. Loretta's remains were recovered from the bay twenty years ago, a few weeks after she died. Five years ago, Esther's remains were recovered from a shallow grave in Calaveras County. The sisters were together the night they vanished. We believe they were killed the same night. We know, from his confession and his DNA, that Lafontaine dated Loretta Gomez for approximately six months, and during that time Loretta became pregnant with Lafontaine's child. We have charged Paul Xavier for the murder of Esther Gomez. There is physical evidence linking him to her remains. And we believe Xavier had an accomplice, someone who helped kill Lori."

Mr. Caddel said, "We're not here to dispute facts."

"Excellent. In addition, during the search of Sheriff Lafontaine's home and storage unit, we discovered an item that belonged to Lori, a red scarf." Pausing, I studied Lafontaine's face. He tried to show he was unfazed, but beads of sweat trickled down his temples, which he quickly wiped away while his eyes remained fixated on the wall behind Martina.

He was sweating all right. "We've since tested the scarf for fluids and particulates. The lab found both Lori and Sheriff Lafontaine's DNA on the scarf."

Mr. Caddel stated, "They were dating. That's not unusual."

I continued, "The last night Lori and Este were seen alive, they took photos. Their aunt developed the film after they went missing. In the photo, Lori and Este were wearing matching red scarves. Este's red scarf was found with her remains. We found the other in your client's storage unit."

Martina pulled out a copy of the photo of Lori and Este wearing the scarves and slid it across the table.

That got Lafontaine's attention. He glanced down at the twins, and his face paled.

Martina glared at Lafontaine. "Yes, that's right. She was so excited about meeting you that night that she took a photo with her sister. The film was time stamped to the night they disappeared."

Martina sat smugly with her arms folded across her chest. Lafontaine turned and whispered to his lawyer.

We sat there in silence as they whispered back and forth for at least a full minute. Once they'd come up with the plan, presumably, Lafontaine said, "I admit I was dating Lori, like you said, and that she was pregnant with my child. I saw Lori the night she went missing. We had met because we were going to talk about the future. The future of us and our baby. Lori had told me she wanted to get rid of the baby, and she wanted to break up with me because I was too much of a reminder of that event. She gave me her scarf to remember her by. She ran off crying. I never saw her after that."

Martina cried out, "Bull crap!"

After I put my hand on Martina's shoulder and gave her a

look to back off the sheriff, I turned to him and said, "You must see how that seems a bit convenient for you. She broke up with you and gave you her scarf as a souvenir. Why would she do that when she and her sister had a matching set that their aunt gave them the previous Christmas? I don't buy it. I think you lured Lori to that bridge. And it was you who tried to convince her to get rid of the baby, and when she refused, you killed her. And your son."

Sheriff's eyes popped before looking down at the ground.

He didn't know the baby was a boy.

Mr. Caddel said, "We've answered your questions. Sheriff Lafontaine told you how he had the scarf in his possession. It's all perfectly innocent. My client has done nothing wrong."

Lafontaine looked back at me and then at Martina. Martina said, "One more question. Why did you keep her scarf after all these years?"

It was a good question. And I'd love an answer.

"I think we're done here," Mr. Caddel declared.

I said, "You said he'd answer all reasonable questions. I'm curious as well. Why did you keep Lori's scarf? You never saw her again, and she never contacted you again. So, I guess I have two questions. One, did you find it strange that you never heard from Lori again? And why did you keep her scarf for twenty years?"

Lafontaine stared directly at me. "I wasn't surprised she didn't contact me again. She broke up with me. She didn't want to see me anymore."

Lies. "And why did you keep her scarf? It's been twenty years."

Lafontaine looked away again.

And then it hit me. But it was puzzling. I said, "You loved her."

Lafontaine didn't meet my gaze.

225

Mr. Caddel said, "And now we're done."

With that, the sheriff stood up, and Mr. Caddel led him out of the room.

When they were out of earshot, and the door was shut, I turned to Martina. "Maybe it was an accident."

"Maybe. But I certainly don't buy the story that she broke up with him that night."

"I don't either."

The door opened, and Sarge and Greggs walked in. We gave them a summary of what had just happened and my latest theory. "An accident. I could see that. But then, why did Xavier kill Este?"

What would I do if I accidentally killed the woman I loved? I would be sick. There was no way I would then murder her sister. "Maybe Lafontaine was distraught over Lori, and Xavier was with him. Xavier knew it would implicate him or at least soil his family name, so they came up with a plan to silence the only witness. Este."

"It's compelling."

Martina added, "Even if it was an accident, Lafontaine was lying through his teeth. And he's a piece of garbage."

No love lost between Martina and Lafontaine. Not that I didn't agree. Lafontaine was lying, and we were going to prove it.

42

HIRSCH

If this were two months ago, I would have been thrilled the team had solved another case. But this one was bittersweet. How do you celebrate that you have found and identified the remains of a ten-year-old boy who had been subjected to a monster and then buried under his house, two blocks from Gerald's home? The worst part of it was how long it took for us to find him.

On the surface, it seemed like the original investigators did everything they could to find Gerald. But they had opted to do it all themselves. If they had brought in the FBI earlier, maybe they would have found him alive or five years ago. Anything would have been better than having to explain to the boy's parents he had been dead and buried for too long. "Hey, Hirsch."

Jayda said, "The parents of Gerald Ackerman are here. They've asked to speak with you and Martina since you took the case and helped find him."

I didn't think it was right for Martina and me to take all the credit. "It was Vincent who had the contact with the FBI."

"Well, then they'll probably want to talk to him, too."

"How are they holding up?"

"As expected. Not well. They've just found out their ten-year-old son is dead and has been buried two blocks from them."

A punch to the gut. Suddenly, I felt sick. "Understood." I closed my laptop and stood up.

"Where's Martina?" Jayda asked.

"She went to refill her coffee. She should be back any minute. I'll grab Vincent too."

Standing there thinking about what I was going to say to Gerald Ackerman's parents, I realized it was the first time since I learned I was going to be a father that I would have to face a child victim's parents. Maybe that was why this one felt different. It had been eight weeks since I learned Kim was pregnant, but I already thought of that little guy or girl daily and hourly. What if one day I was on the receiving end of what I was about to say? How did Martina do this job? She was tough for sure. She had a ten-year-old girl, yet she investigated dozens of child cases, missing persons and homicide. The works.

Martina strolled in with a steaming cup of coffee. "Hey, what's up?"

"Gerald Ackerman's family is here and wants to speak with us." I called out, "Hey, Vincent."

He ran over. "Hey."

"Gerald Ackerman's family is here and wants to speak with us. You too."

Vincent paled. "Me too?"

"They want to thank us. You were pivotal in finding Gerald."

"Oh, okay."

We walked quietly down to one of the conference rooms. Jayda opened the door, and I walked in. Martina and Vincent followed me. The air was thick with grief.

Ross sat across from Mrs. Ackerman, who had shoulder-length brown hair and blue eyes filled with tears. Mr. Ackerman sat next to her, his arm around her. The resemblance to their child was unmistakable. "Mr. and Mrs. Ackerman."

They stood up. Mr. Ackerman said, "Detective. Ms. Monroe."

"This is Vincent, a member of the team who was pivotal in the case."

Mr. Ackerman said, "It's nice to meet you, Vincent."

Vincent shook their hands. I supposed I could have prepped him for his first victim's family meeting.

Mr. Ackerman said, "Thank you. All of you. I don't know how you did it. We had hired private investigators, and the police had worked tirelessly. How did you find our son so quickly?"

"Well, as my detectives may have told you, we're the Cold Case Squad. So, unlike the homicide team, we don't just look at what needs to be done to find someone, but we look at the case file and see what wasn't done that should've been, and sometimes that's enough to break a case wide open. In this case, that's what we did. The original investigators did a fine job of interviewing everyone, which usually can lead to a suspect. But in this case, it hadn't, so we brought in an FBI profiler to help us narrow down what our suspect may look like, his demographic, his background, and where he may live. The FBI profiler created the profile and could match it up to one person interviewed during the original investigation. From there, Jayda and Ross ran with it and found your son. It was a group effort. And I am sorry for your loss."

Martina added, "I'm sorry for your loss."

Vincent whispered the same.

"Thank you. Thank all of you. Not knowing was so, so awful, yet there was hope too, you know, but I just..." Mrs. Ackerman broke down into sobs.

Something happened to me at that moment. My eyes

watered and my nose tingled. My throat felt dry. I glanced at Martina, who stood stoically next to me. How did she do it?

"Is there anything we can do for you, Mr. And Mrs. Ackerman?" Martina asked.

"No. Thank you again."

I glanced over at Ross and Jayda and then motioned for Martina and Vincent to exit.

Jayda and Ross had taken over the investigation while we were busy trying to figure out how to ensure the Gomez sisters' murderers were sent to prison.

Halfway down the hall, I sniffled and ran my fingers through my hair. Martina stopped and put her hand on my shoulder to stop me. "You okay?"

"I don't know how you do it."

"What do you mean?"

"You're a parent. How do you not wrap Zoey in bubble wrap and put her under twenty-four-hour surveillance?"

Martina smiled. "It's not easy. Especially with what we see and what we do and the families we talk to. But you have to go in knowing that at some point you have to let go. Eventually, they're old enough to go to school and be away from you all day while they're at school. And then eventually they go places without you, like a friend's house or to the movies. I'm not sure how teenagers work, and I'm not looking forward to it." She shook her head. "I guess the short answer is, you just do. We brought their son back to them. Unfortunately, not the way we wanted to, but they have him. And they can bury him. They can remember him. That's our gift to the family."

Parenthood seemed so much tougher than I had envisioned. When I told people my wife was expecting a baby, they were overjoyed for us, with congratulations all around. What about the devastating parts of parenthood? What if someone took my child or Zoey? I wasn't sure I could cope.

When my brother was murdered, we didn't question whether he was dead or alive. We didn't have that uncertainty. Not that it made it easier, I supposed. Perhaps parenthood was taking the joy along with the heartbreak. The worry and near panic every moment that child wasn't near you. "I suppose you'll help me through it."

"You'll do fine, Hirsch. You'll do more than fine. You'll be a brilliant father. But yes, you will worry and be overprotective."

"Thanks. That's some heavy stuff."

"Yeah, and it's only Wednesday. We still need to figure out a way to nail Lafontaine."

Wasn't that the truth? We reached the squad room, but before I entered, my phone buzzed. Panic set in. Was there something wrong with Kim? I pulled out my cell and said, "It's Greggs. Hello."

"I have an early Christmas present for you."

A small smile formed. "I love presents."

"Paul Xavier wants to make a deal. He's ready to talk."

Nearly speechless, I eyed Martina and said, "Tell us when and where. We'll be there."

43

MARTINA

Paul Xavier sat with his lawyer, wearing a smug look on his face. He was only going to serve twenty years for killing Esther Gomez and every other crime he had committed. His lawyer and the DA had worked out a deal. In exchange for Xavier's full cooperation, in all cases, he would only receive twenty years in jail. He could have murdered ten people and he would only get twenty years in jail. In twenty years, Paul Xavier would be sixty-two years old and would be free to hug his children and grandchildren. I didn't like it, but it would be the only way to get Lafontaine. Would it be worth it?

We were about to find out.

Sitting around the large conference room table were Paul Xavier's lawyer, District Attorney Greggs, Hirsch, and myself. The cameras were rolling.

Hirsch said, "There are multiple cases that we would like to talk to you about today."

Paul said, "I'll tell you everything I know."

I nodded. "Let's start with Loretta and Esther Gomez. Tell us everything you know about their disappearance and their deaths. Start from the beginning, please."

232

Paul fidgeted in his chair.

His lawyer gave him a reassuring nod.

I had zero sympathy for him. He earned the hot seat.

Paul began. "Frederick Lafontaine and I have known each other since second grade. We were best friends. He started dating a girl, Lori. I had never met her before, but he told me about her. He said she was Hispanic and so he didn't want to bring her around his family or his friends. From my understanding, it bothered him quite a bit because he cared for her. He actually said he loved her, which I thought was crazy at the time." He sipped on his water.

Apparently, rolling on your best friend to save your own butt made you thirsty.

He continued, "From what he told me, he told his parents about Lori. They were not happy and told him to break up with her or he'd be cut off. So, he broke up with her. But then she calls and they meet. Lori tells Freddie she's pregnant. He freaks out and tells his parents. They tell him under no circumstances is Lori to have the baby. He gets back together to get her to have an abortion. He thinks if he can convince her they will be together, she'll agree to get rid of the baby."

Disgusted, I sighed loudly.

"Believe it or not, in his own way, he loved her, and he fought his parents. His parents won. They gave Freddie $10,000 to give to Lori in exchange for her to have an abortion."

I thought I was going to be sick. And if what Xavier said was true, I thought Lafontaine's parents should be prosecuted along with him and this scumbag. "So, Lafontaine's parents were bribing Lori to end the pregnancy?"

"Yes."

Hirsch said, "Then what happened?"

"Freddie got the cash, and we were going to meet her to make the proposition."

"I need to stop you. Just out of curiosity. He loved her, but he was willing to bribe her to have an abortion?"

"Yes, like I said. He loved her as much as he could love her under the circumstances."

I shook my head, in no way able to fathom this situation. "And if she had agreed to end the pregnancy, would he have continued dating her?"

"I don't know. We really didn't get that far into the plan. But I think he knew he didn't have a future with her. Not with his family. They wouldn't allow a Hispanic in the family. At least not back then. It was a different time."

Hirsch said, "You gathered the $10,000 to bribe Lori. And then what happened?"

"Freddie, Frederick Lafontaine, asked me to go with him to talk to Lori. Not to actually talk with her, but to be there in case he needed backup. I think he was scared of how Lori would react. He asked Lori to meet on the bridge in Alameda where they went on a date or something. It was symbolic. The plan was for me to stay in the car when he met her."

It was disgusting.

"And you stayed in the car?"

"No. But I stayed near the car smoking a cigarette."

"And then?"

"Freddie walked up to the bridge, and I waited at the entrance smoking a cigarette. Everything seemed fine for a while and then they argued. She was yelling and crying. So, I ran up to see what was going on."

"What did you see?"

"Lori was pounding at Freddie's chest and crying, saying she couldn't believe he would do this to her. She pushes him, and by this point, Freddie is frantic and yelling back that she just needs to get it done, and he grabs her by the shoulders. She fought him and he picked her up. She was a lot smaller than

Freddie. It looked like he was trying to calm her, but she was flailing around, and he lost his grip on her. And the next thing I knew, there was a scream, and Freddie was leaning over the railing, and then I heard the splash. I ran up to see what happened and Freddie stood there frozen with a red scarf in his hands. The screaming continued, and that's when I realized there was another person there. I had never seen her before. But she was screaming at Freddie, and he said it was an accident."

"That was Este?"

"Yes, I learned her name later."

"Did Freddie know Este would be there?"

"No."

"And then what happened?"

"Este was screaming for Lori. Freddie was crying and saying he didn't know what happened. He grabbed her by the scarf to catch her, but it was no use. I told him he needed to snap out of it. Este said we had to get help. Freddie agreed, but I knew the implications. If the press found out I was there and Freddie killed Lori, our lives were over. I told Freddie we had to get rid of Este."

Dang.

"Freddie didn't agree at first. But then I put my hand over Este's mouth to quiet her, and then I dragged her to the car. I put her in the trunk and used her scarf to quiet her. And we sat in the car. Freddie was a wreck. I told him we had to get rid of Este and that if it ever got out what happened, our lives and our family's lives would be ruined."

"And then what happened?"

"Freddie finally came around to the reality of the situation and agreed. He said we could go up to his parents' house in Arnold."

"In Calaveras County?"

"Yes. And then he realized their car must be parked nearby.

H.K. CHRISTIE

Freddie went to the trunk and got the keys from Este. Back in the car, we drove around looking for Este and Lori's car. When we found it, Freddie decided he would drive it and follow me to Arnold."

My stomach grew queasy at the thought that Este had to witness Lori's murder and then was taken hostage.

"What happened next?"

"When we arrived in Arnold, I carried Este out behind the cabin. Freddie was right behind me. I told him to strangle her, but he couldn't. He was a wreck. So, I threw her on the ground and used her scarf to strangle her. But it was taking too long, and she was fighting me. Freddie handed me a pocketknife, and I remember that moment because I looked up at him, and he had tears in his eyes. He was always too soft. I then stabbed Este's chest and neck until she stopped moving, and it was obvious she was dead. Freddie had a shovel from his parents' cabin, and we dug a grave, put Este inside, and filled it up."

I looked at Hirsch, who was as disturbed as I was. It was hard not to be. "And what did you do next?"

"We went inside Freddie's parents' cabin and cleaned up. I was covered in blood, so I showered, and then we burned our clothes. I told Freddie not to worry, I had family in the police department. And if we were smart, we wouldn't get caught."

Lafontaine wasn't a psychopath like Xavier, but he was a monster all the same.

"And who was it who helped you cover this up, and how did they do it?"

The lawyer looked to Paul sternly, as if willing him to continue. Even after his murderous confession, he didn't want to roll on his own family. "My cousin David was working missing persons. I told him he was likely to get a report of missing twins and to make sure that he took it. And when their aunt came in to report her nieces missing, he took the report and labeled them runaways and didn't put them in the missing persons database."

"Did he do anything else to cover up that crime?"

"That was it."

"Did he know that you and Lafontaine had murdered two women?"

"I didn't give any details. He knew better than to ask."

Because he knew Paul was a psychopath? What else had he done?

Hirsch turned to DA Greggs. "Is that enough to convict Lafontaine?"

"It is. Assuming, of course, Mr. Xavier follows the stipulations of the plea deal, which means he will testify to all of this in open court."

Hirsch turned back to Xavier. "What happened to the pocketknife?"

"The next day, we took Este and Lori's car to Discovery Bay and rolled it into the water. After that, we threw in the pocketknife."

If it weren't for Xavier's publicity stunt to submit his DNA into CODIS, Frederick Lafontaine and Xavier would've gotten away with a double murder. They were smart, but not smart enough.

Hirsch turned the page in his notebook. "The next case we have to ask you about is Richard Whitlock's murder."

Paul Xavier nodded. His cousin had obviously informed him we had connected him to the crime. "Richard Whitlock worked for me. He was a decent enough guy, or so I thought. After work one night, we went to a bar like we often did. I had a few too many shots of tequila. Somehow, we got on the topic of twins, and it slipped out I'd once known twins, but they were dead now, and I guess I said something to insinuate I killed them. To be honest, I'm not exactly sure what I said, but the next day, Richard Whitlock confronted me and said that he would tell the press I killed the twins if I didn't pay him off."

"Richard Whitlock was blackmailing you?"

"Yes."

"Did you give him any money?"

"I did. To the tune of eight million before I realized the blackmail wouldn't stop."

"So then, what did you do?"

"A friend of my cousin knew a hired gun he met on the job. I hired him to kill Richard. The night Richard was to be killed, I told him I needed to talk to him about the payments and to meet me at the park. I didn't meet him at the park. It was the hired gun. I don't even know his name. I never met him. They did all the transactions through David."

"Richard Whitlock wasn't embezzling money from your company?"

"No, but that was how we covered up the loss of the eight million that I used to pay him. So, in a way, he had embezzled it, but it was through me."

Interesting way of rationalizing the situation.

"Your cousin David Xavier hired the hitman?" Hirsch asked.

"Yes."

"That constitutes conspiracy to commit murder."

Xavier shrugged. "I'm sure he knew that. He was a police officer."

What a piece of work.

Hirsch said to DA Greggs, "Do we have enough for David Xavier to be arrested on conspiracy to commit murder, as well as covering a crime?"

"Right now it's hearsay, but we can look at David's records and see if we can corroborate the story. And we can bring him in again and ask him about it."

Paul said, "He'll never admit to it."

Hirsch leaned over and whispered to me, "Anything else you want to ask?"

I whispered back. "No, but I really want to go and arrest Lafontaine."

A small smile crept up Hirsch's face. "We're done here."

44

MARTINA

The sky was blue with the sun shining down on the Gomez family and the hundreds of people who gathered to remember Este and Lori. When we opened up the twins' missing persons file, I hadn't realized the impact its conclusion would have.

The sisters were missing for twenty years without a peep, but Hirsch and I knew better than to give up on them. We didn't and wouldn't have stopped digging until we found them. We used our experience and our instincts, and we were successful. One thing they can't teach in the police academy or on-the-job or in the classroom is instinct. Hirsch noticed right away that there was something fishy about the case when he recognized the name Xavier.

We found the truth about what had happened to Loretta and Esther Gomez. It was sad, and it was sickening. And I didn't think justice was fully served. The former sheriff, Frederick Lafontaine, was charged with two counts of second-degree murder and had opted for a deal instead of going through with a trial. He would serve twenty-five years with a possibility for parole after twenty. Paul Xavier would serve twenty years for his role. Was it enough?

No one else was charged for cover-ups or contributing to the Gomez sisters' deaths. Unfortunately, there was nothing that pointed to David Xavier hiring a contract killer or assisting in any coverups other than he hadn't input the girls' names into the missing persons database. The Richard Whitlock case was closed, with the blame only lying with Paul Xavier. The DA thought the case against David Xavier was flimsy, and he was right, but it didn't seem right that David Xavier remained a free person. I hoped Paul Xavier and Lafontaine were miserable for every single day of their sentences. They were supposed to serve and protect, and they not only failed to do that but did the complete opposite.

If I ran the universe, I would have also charged Frederick Lafontaine's parents as accessories to the twins' murders. I believe that if they hadn't pushed him to break up with and bribe Lori, nobody would have ended up dead.

Hate should never win.

Last I checked, I didn't run the world, so we had to accept the justice system's decision to only prosecute Paul Xavier and Frederick Lafontaine.

Did I feel good about watching Hirsch cuff Lafontaine? You bet. When we arrested him, he didn't seem surprised, but he seemed sad. I asked him if he really loved Lori, but he wouldn't answer. Even after being charged with her murder, he didn't want people to know he had loved somebody who didn't look like his family or his relatives. He was a disgrace to the badge and to our community. I was relieved he was no longer the sheriff of CoCo County.

With Lafontaine in prison, the interim sheriff's role fell to Sarge, who was more than ready for the special election to be held so he could go back to just being Sarge. He was clear he didn't want the job. He only accepted the role to keep the department afloat. But between you and me, Mom loved bragging that she was dating the sheriff.

As one would imagine, the press was all over this. Not only was it nightly news for weeks that the sheriff and mayor were charged with murder, but when child killer Trent Blackwell was arrested for the death of Gerald Ackerman, we were practically household names again. One reporter had suggested they rename the Cold Case Squad, The Hot Case Squad. It was silly, but it had been a heck of a week.

Although Trent Blackwell was arrested, the teams were still collecting evidence from his home to ensure that he got the maximum sentence for Gerald's death and to determine if he had taken any other children. The DA was pretty confident he would get the max sentence for Gerald's death.

As much as Hirsch and I and the rest of the squad had tried our best to avoid the press, it was inevitable. They were everywhere and there were a lot of them. Finally, we agreed to a press conference, led by our media liaison. We answered questions the best we could and hoped people would forget our faces and our names soon because we weren't the stars. We weren't the people who needed the attention. It was the missing, the murdered, and the exploited who needed the attention, like Lori and Este Gomez had needed our attention twenty years earlier. And that was exactly what we told them. We hadn't expected the reaction from the public that came after.

As I squeezed my little girl's hand, I admired my family and close friends and hundreds of strangers. The entire Cold Case Squad was in attendance with their spouses to remember the lives of Loretta and Esther Gomez. It wasn't just us who attended her memorial. Besides a handful of family members, hundreds of others, who had never met Lori or Este, had gathered that day wearing T-shirts with the girls' photo, from the last night wearing their matching red scarves, that read, "Gone but not forgotten."

The Cold Case Squad and I saw the worst of humanity. It was refreshing to see the other side for a change. The side where complete strangers showed up for sisters who had been tossed aside and covered up. Strangers demanding for Lori and Este to be seen. To be valued. To be remembered. Not only that, but to remind the rest of the world that no matter the color of your skin, you are important, valuable, and deserving of love.

ALSO BY H.K. CHRISTIE

The Martina Monroe Series is a nail-biting suspense series starring Private Investigator Martina Monroe. If you like high-stakes games, jaw-dropping twists, and embattled seekers struggling to do right, then you'll love H.K. Christie's thrilling series.

What She Left, **Martina Monroe, PI, Book 1**

She's on her last chance. When the bodies start piling up, she'll need to save more than her job.

Martina Monroe is a single bad day away from losing it all. Stuck catching insurance fraudsters and cheating spouses due to a DUI, the despondent PI yearns to return to more fulfilling gigs. So when a prospective client asks for her by name to identify an unknown infant in a family photo, she leaps at the opportunity and travels to the one place she swore never to go: back home.

As the pressure mounts and the temptation of booze calls like a siren, Martina digs into the mystery and discovers many of the threads have razor-sharp ends. And forced to partner with a resentful detective investigating a linked suspicious death, the haunted private eye unravels clues that delve deep into her past... and put her in a dark and dangerous corner.

Can this gritty detective unlock the truth before she's drowned in a sea of secrets?

If She Ran, **Martina Monroe, PI, Book 2**

Three months. Three missing women. One PI

determined to discover the truth.

Back from break, PI Martina Monroe clears the air with her boss at Drakos Security & Investigations and is ready to jump right into solving cold cases for the CoCo County Sheriff's Department.

Diving into the cold case files Martina stumbles upon a pattern of missing young women, all of whom were deemed runaways, and the files froze with minimal detective work from the original investigators. The more Martina digs into the women's last days the more shocking discoveries she makes.

Soon, Martina and Detective Hirsch not only uncover additional missing women but when their star witness turns up dead, they must rush to the next before it's too late.

A gripping, unputdownable thriller full of mystery and suspense.

All She Wanted, **Martina Monroe, PI, Book 3**

A tragic death. A massive cover-up. PI Martina Monroe must face her past in order to reveal the truth.

PI Martina Monroe has found her groove working cold cases alongside Detective Hirsch at the CoCo County Sheriff's Department. With a growing team of cold case detectives, Martina and Hirsch are on the heels of bringing justice for Julie DeSoto - a woman Martina failed to protect one year earlier. But when Martina receives a haunting request from her past, it nearly tears her in two.

As Julie's case turns hot, so does the investigation into a young soldier's untimely death. As both cases rattle Martina to the core, she now questions everything she believed about her time working for Drakos Security & Investigations and with the United States Army. Martina must uncover the truth for her sanity and her own life.

Pushed to the brink, Martina risks everything to expose the real criminals and bring justice for the victim's family and her own.

A gripping, page-turning thriller, full of suspense.

***Why She Lied*, Martina Monroe, PI, Book 4**

A missing mother and child. A secret past revealed. Will Martina and Hirsch discover the truth before they meet their end?

In the thick of the current cold case investigation, PI Martina Monroe receives a hand-written letter from a desperate mother pleading for Martina and Hirsch to reopen the cold case of the woman's missing daughter and five-year-old grandson. Feeling a deep connection to the request, Martina knows that Hirsch and she have found their next case.

As the two investigators dig into the life of Ana and her son, Ryder, they quickly find Ana has the life many would be envious of. With a loving group of family and friends, a devoted husband, and a successful career, Ana's perfect life seems a bit too perfect for Martina and Hirsch.

Searching even further into Ana's past, they find a startling secret that leads Martina and Hirsch into the dark world of organized crime. Hot on the trail, the two investigators head to New York City, hoping to find the answer to what happened to Ana and Ryder. However, as soon as they touch down, they realize they aren't the only ones on the hunt.

Will Martina and Hirsch discover the truth before they become victims themselves?

***Secrets She Kept*, Martina Monroe, PI, Book 5**

A ritualistic murder. Multiple suspects. Can the cold

case detectives find the truth before the killers strike again?

Ten years earlier, two teenage girls were found murdered by what appeared to be a satanic sacrifice. The case had dominated the news headlines for months before the original investigators failed to arrest the perpetrators of the crime - despite multiple suspects. Without solid evidence to prosecute, and even with the near-heroic efforts of the original detectives, the homicide investigation turned cold. For years, the families of the two victims fought to keep the young women's memory alive and to get the attention of law enforcement to not give up on finding those responsible.

In an election year, and with a stellar record for the CoCo County Sheriff's Department Cold Case Squad, the Sheriff hands cold case investigators Martina Monroe and Detective Hirsch the most notorious decade-old murder case - named by the press, 'The Twin Satan Murders.' Unlike most of their previous cold cases, The Twin Satan Murders were thoroughly investigated by previous detectives. Undeterred by the lack of evidence and answers from the original investigation, Martina and Hirsch investigate the murders as if it were day one.

Knocking on doors, Martina and Hirsch are surprised by the lack of cooperation from the original witnesses. With pushback from the community, the two investigators are forced to dive into the world of the occult. What the two detectives find is more disturbing than any case they've worked on before. Soon, Martina and Detective Hirsch find that some powerful people will go to all lengths to keep the truth buried.

Will Martina and Detective Hirsch find the actual killers before they become victims themselves?

What She Found, **Martina Monroe, PI, Book 6**

A ritualistic murder. Multiple suspects. Can the cold case detectives find the truth before the killers strike again?

A missing woman. A chilling connection to a baby trafficking ring. Will the Cold Case Investigators stop the killers before another woman is taken?

Martina and Detective Hirsch, still reeling from their last high-profile case, agree to reopen the missing person case of Sadie Jarreau, a friend of one member of the Cold Case Squad. At first glance, Sadie's disappearance from the local marina looks like the typical unhappy marriage resulting in a deadly end. But between the marina's surveillance cameras malfunctioning that day, her husband's air-tight alibi, and no one with a motive to harm Sadie, Martina and Hirsch are forced to consider a less common scenario - a stranger abduction.

As they pursue the possibility that a stranger took Sadie, Martina and Hirsch stumble onto a string of sinister crimes that occurred shortly before, and after, Sadie went missing. Digging deep into the case files of murdered pregnant women found on the Northern California Coast, with their unborn children missing, the team makes a terrible realization.

Whoever had been kidnapping young, pregnant women and removing their children before dumping their bodies in the bay - had not stopped. Now it is up to Hirsch and Martina to dive into the world of baby trafficking to find those responsible and bring them to justice.

Will they stop the killers before another woman is taken?

What She Found is the sixth installment of the Martina Monroe thriller series.

How She Fell, **Martina Monroe, PI, Book 7**

Missing twin sisters. A chilling revelation. Will this be

the case that breaks the Cold Case Squad?

Twenty years earlier, a set of female eighteen-year-old twins went missing in the Bay Area. There were no news reports or national coverage. The original investigators had barely touched the case, and like so many other cases of missing teens, were quickly labeled runaways, and the file sat on the shelf. Baffled by the lack of attention for the sisters, Martina insists it will be Hirsch and the Cold Case Squad's next case.

Undeterred by the lack of prior research, the team dives into the case, employing methods of investigation and forensic technology not available twenty years earlier. This could be the case where time is actually on their side. When the team catches their first big break, the discovery of one sister's remains, and a lead on the second, they shift the case from missing persons to homicide.

With the change in course, Martina and Hirsch dig deeper into the women's lives before they disappeared. With a no-stone-unturned approach and DNA results back from the lab, they soon find a shocking connection to one of their own. Concerned the information could jeopardize getting justice for the victims' family, Martina and Hirsch now must work in the shadows in order to find answers to what happened all those years ago.

Will Martina and Hirsch be able to expose the truth without endangering themselves, their jobs, and the future of the Cold Case Squad?

Her Last Words, **Martina Monroe Book 8**

Release date: April 28, 2023

A string of puzzling murders. A skilled and dangerous killer. Will the Cold Case Squad discover the truth in time to save one of their own?

PI Martina Monroe and Detective Hirsch accept the new sheriff's request to reopen a ten-year-old murder case. Not that they could refuse. The victim was the sheriff's brother, a married father of two.

As the team digs in, they find two nearly identical murders. In all three cases there were no suspects and no motive. The only connection is their profession and cause of death. The links are thin, but Martina and Hirsch know better than to ignore them.

With few leads to go on, Martina and Hirsch hold a press conference to garner the attention of the public and ask for anyone with information to come forward. Even as the tips roll in, the team is left with no new leads.

Frustrated, Martina and Hirsch start from scratch and begin pounding the pavement to interview family, friends, and coworkers until Martina receives a tip. Not a tip.

A warning.

Undeterred by the threat against her and the squad, Martina calls for an all-hands on deck to solve the case. Will the squad discover the truth before one of their own pays the ultimate price?

The Selena Bailey Series is a suspenseful series featuring a young Selena Bailey and her turbulent path to becoming a top notch kick-ass private investigator as led by her mentor, Martina Monroe.

Not Like Her, **Selena Bailey, Book 1**

A battered mother. A possessive boyfriend. Can she save herself from a similar fate?

Selena longs to flee her uneasy home life. Prepping every spare minute for a college escape, the headstrong, high school senior vows never to be like her alcoholic mom with her string of abusive boyfriends. So when Selena finds her beaten nearly to death, she knows safety is slipping away...

With her mother's violent lover evading justice, Selena's new boyfriend's offer to move in seems Heaven-sent. But jealous rage and a renewed search for her long-lost father threaten to pull her back into harm's way.

Can Selena break free of an ugly past, or will brutal men crush her hopes of a better future?

Not Like Her is the first book in the suspenseful Selena Bailey series. If you like thrilling twists, dark tension, and smart and driven women, then you'll love H.K. Christie's new dark mystery series.

Trigger warning: This book includes themes relating to domestic violence

---

One In Five, Selena Bailey, Book 2

A predator running free and the girl determined to stop him.

After escaping a violent past, Selena Bailey, starts her first semester of college determined to put it all behind her - until her roommate is attacked at the Delta Kappa Alpha house. After reporting the attack, police refuse to prosecute due to lack of evidence, claiming another case of 'he said, she said'.

As Selena and Dee begin meeting other victims, it's clear Dee's assault wasn't an isolated event. Selena determined to take down the DKA house, takes matters into her own hands in order to claim justice for Dee and prevent the next attack.

Will Selena get justice for the women of SFU or will she become the next victim?

On The Rise, Selena Bailey, Book 3

A little girl is taken. A mysterious cover-up. One young investigator determined to find the truth.

Selena Bailey, a sophomore at the local university studying criminal justice, returns from winter break to jump into her first official case as a private investigator with her stepmother's security firm.

Thrown into an undercover detail, Selena soon discovers a much darker plot. What seemed like a tragic kidnapping is revealed to be just the tip of the iceberg. Will Selena expose the truth before not only the little girl's life, but her own is lost forever?

Go With Grace, **Selena Bailey, Book 4**

A dangerous stalker. A desperate classmate. Will one young investigator risk everything to help a stranger in need?

Selena Bailey returns in her senior year of college determined to keep her head down and out of other people's lives with the sole intent of keeping them safe and out of harm's way.

Selena is focused more than ever, with three major goals: graduate with her bachelor's degree in Criminal Justice, obtain her Private Investigator's license and find her late boyfriend, Brendon's, killers.

Her plans are derailed when a desperate classmate approaches Selena for her help. At first, she refuses but Dillon is certain his life is in danger and provides Selena with proof. With no one else to turn to, Selena reluctantly takes the case.

The investigation escalates quickly as Selena soon discovers the woman stalking Dillon is watching his, and now Selena's, every move.

Will Selena be able to save Dillon's life and her own?

***Flawless*, Selena Bailey, Book 5**

A young woman clinging on to life. A desperate family fighting for answers. Will Selena be able to discover the truth in time to save her?

Selena Bailey returns with her Private Investigator license in one hand and the first official case for Bailey Investigations in the other.

When the sister of a young woman, fighting for her life in the Intensive Care Unit, pleads with Selena to explore her sister, Stephanie's, last days before she slipped into a coma, Selena must go undercover in the billion dollar beauty industry to discover the truth.

The deeper Selena delves into Stephanie's world, the more she fears for Stephanie's life and so many others.

As Selena unravels the truth behind an experimental weight loss regimen, she finds it's not only weight the good doctor's patients are losing. Selena now must rush against the clock to save not only Stephanie's life, but her own.

A Permanent Mark: A heartless killer. Weeks without answers. Can she move on when a murderer walks free?

Kendall Murphy's life comes crashing to a halt at the news her husband has been killed in a tragic hit-and-run. Devastated and out-of-sorts, she can't seem to come to terms with the senselessness of it all. Despite, promises by a young detective, she fears they'll never find the person responsible for her husband's death.

As months go by without answers, Kendall, with the help of her grandmother and sister, deals with her grief as she tries to create a new life for herself. But when the detective discovers that the death was a murder-for-hire, suddenly everyone from her new love interest and those closest to her are under suspicion. And it may only be a matter of time before the assassin strikes again...

Can Kendall trust anyone, or will misplaced loyalty make her the next victim?

If you like riveting suspense and gripping mysteries then you'll love *A Permanent Mark* - starring a grown up Selena Bailey.

THANK YOU!

Thank you for reading *How She Fell*. I hope you enjoyed reading it as much as I loved writing it. If you did, I would greatly appreciate if you could post a short review.

Reviews are crucial for any author and can make a huge difference in visibility of current and future works. Reviews allow us to continue doing what we love, *writing stories*. Not to mention, I would be forever grateful!

Thank you!

JOIN H.K. CHRISTIE'S READER CLUB

Join my reader club to be the first to hear about upcoming novels, new releases, giveaways, promotions, as well as, a free e-copy of the **prequel to the Martina Monroe series**, *Crashing Down.*

It's completely free to sign up and you'll never be spammed by me, you can opt out easily at any time.

Sign up at
www.authorhkchristie.com

ABOUT THE AUTHOR

H. K. Christie watched horror films far too early in life. Inspired by the likes of Stephen King, true crime podcasts, and a vivid imagination she now writes suspenseful thrillers featuring unbreakable women.

When not working on her latest novel, she can be found eating & drinking with friends, walking around the lakes, or playing with her favorite furry pal.

She is a native and current resident of the San Francisco Bay Area.

www.authorhkchristie.com

ACKNOWLEDGMENTS

Listening to my favorite true crime podcast, Crime Junkie, I heard the story of twin sisters Jeannette and Dannette Millbrook who went missing in 1990 from Augusta, GA. They were just fifteen years old, but like many missing teens, were quickly deemed runaways by the police. Decades later the case received attention from the podcasting community and it shed light on the injustices they faced and mishandling of the case (like removing them from the missing persons database!!!). The details are *maddening*. I encourage you to listen to the podcast or look up the case. The sisters have never been found. If you have any information about the case, you can submit information here: https://www.themillbrooktwins.com/

Jeannette and Dannette's story stuck with me and inspired the latest Martina and Hirsch investigation.

Many thanks to the Crime Junkie team who continue to try to help find the missing by sharing the stories and donating to organizations to help bring answers to their families.

And...some of the details in the story were also inspired by my favorite musical artist, Taylor Swift. More specifically from my favorite song, *All Too Well* (*10 minute version*), that features a woman 'kept like a secret', heartbreak, and a certain scarf 'he' held on to because it smelled like 'her'. Of course, because I'm a thriller author when I hear 'smell' I think 'perfume molecules... skin cells...sweat... *DNA evidence.*'

In the case of Lori's former love, Freddie Lafontaine, I think we can all agree, he most definitely regrets keeping her old scarf.

Taylor, if you're reading this, thank you for your gorgeous music and beautiful soul.

To the rest of you, yeah, yeah. The likelihood she is reading this is a long shot. But you have to remember, I live in a fantasy world in which I create fiction every day and can write any story I want. Even one where Taylor Swift reads my books. And...um, thank you for reading my books. It's most appreciated. Without you I couldn't continue doing what I love - writing stories.

I would also like to extend my deepest gratitude to my Advanced Reader Team. My ARC Team is invaluable in taking the first look at my stories and spreading awareness of my stories through their reviews and kind words. To my editor Paula Lester, a huge thank you for your careful edits and helpful comments. And many thanks to my proof reader, Becky Stewart. To my cover designer, Odile, thank you for your guidance and talent. To my husband and my dog, Charlie, thank you for supporting me in every thing I do.

Made in the USA
Monee, IL
03 January 2023

24130117R00156